OTHER
Harlequin Romances
by MARGARET MAYO

1980—DESTINY PARADISE
1996—SHADES OF AUTUMN
2028—PERILOUS WATERS
2051—LAND OF ICE AND FIRE
2086—RAINBOW MAGIC

Many of these titles are available at your local bookseller
or through the Harlequin Reader Service.

For a free catalogue listing all available Harlequin Romances,
send your name and address to:

HARLEQUIN READER SERVICE,
M.P.O. Box 707, Niagara Falls, N.Y. 14302
Canadian address: Stratford, Ontario, Canada N5A 6W4

or use order coupon at back of books.

Sea Gypsy

by

MARGARET MAYO

Harlequin Books

TORONTO • LONDON • NEW YORK • AMSTERDAM • SYDNEY

Original hardcover edition published in 1977
by Mills & Boon Limited

ISBN 0-373-02118-6

Harlequin edition published November 1977

CHAPTER ONE

HE was called the sea gypsy; rarely spending more than a few weeks in his native England at a time when he could be seen painting *Romany II*, repairing the rigging and sails and generally kitting her out for his next voyage.

He did indeed look like a gypsy with his dark, curly hair, swarthy complexion and jet black eyes that seemed to look into your very soul. Since her meeting with him a few weeks ago Jay had been unable to erase his face from her mind. No other man had impressed her in this manner. Not that she did not have many boyfriends—she was very popular with the opposite sex—but this one was different. The sea gypsy was all man, as tough as they come; yet for all that Jay had gained the impression that he was lonely. What was it he had said to her? 'I need no one. I live alone and I like it that way.' But could anyone in all sincerity say that? There must be times when he desired company—whether it was the friendship of another man or the love of a woman. She guessed him to be in his mid-thirties. How much longer would he live in voluntary exile? Did he never intend leading a conventional way of life, or was he determined to carry on sailing the high seas until old age or ill health forced him to give up his incessant wanderings?

As Jay undid the moorings on her brother's boat she tossed these thoughts back and forth in her mind. Her one brief encounter with the owner of *Romany II* had led to many sleepless nights, and now she intended finding out for herself what magic an isolated life at sea held. The *Romany II* had sailed earlier that day. From a discreet distance Jay had watched him go; felt an incomprehensible sadness. It had been three years since he last put into port at Brixham—when she was but fifteen and still at school. In her youthful way she had envied his free-and-easy existence; had thought him some sort of a hero, having heard him described by her parents as a modern adventurer. He had already completed two trips round the world and it was said that this was to be his third attempt.

Jay started the engine and was soon speeding across the harbour towards the open sea. If Rick knew she had taken his boat there would be hell to pay, but he need never find out. She would be back before dark; all she wanted was to satisfy her curiosity. A few hours out of sight of land and people, drifting in absolute silence, would give her some idea of the freedom enjoyed by the sea gypsy, maybe help her to understand the way his mind worked.

Smiling to herself, Jay recalled his expression the day she had asked if he wanted a crew. It had not been her own idea—sailing was a complete mystery to her— but the fact that she had more than once mentioned this man and frequently watched him stitching new sails

6

or repairing rigging had goaded her friends into betting that she could not get a ride on his yacht. Never one to turn down a wager, Jay had immediately accepted.

Dressed in navy flared trousers and white polo jumper, with a nautical cap set at a rakish angle on her raven black hair, Jay had climbed on board the *Romany II*, confident that she looked every inch a seasoned sea traveller. In actual fact a tour of the local coastline was about her limit. Trying to still the sudden pounding of her heart as she approached the dark-skinned gypsy and disregarding his taciturn expression, she had plunged straight in with her carefully rehearsed speech.

'I've been given to understand,' she said, flashing him one of her attractive smiles, 'that you're looking for a crew on your next voyage.' He frowned, but undeterred, Jay carried on, 'I have considerable experience of sailing and I'm sure you'd find me a big help.'

This was when he had said he needed no one. Jay had not been surprised—it confirmed the reports she had heard of the man. She tried again, 'This is a wonderful yacht you have, Mr—er——?' When he made no attempt to speak she shrugged and continued, 'I'm sure she must handle marvellously. Is it true that you've sailed twice round the world in her?'

He carried on stitching a sail with meticulous care and for one moment Jay thought he was going to ignore her question. Then he looked up, his bright, black eyes piercing her own. 'Once,' he amended. 'The time before was in *Romany I*. Now if you don't mind, I have work to do.'

Jay ran her hand admiringly over the gleaming paintwork. 'Wouldn't you consider taking me on a short trip? I mean, it would be wonderful to say I'd been out in the famous *Romany II*.'

He smiled, though there was no humour in the dark eyes. 'You're right, I wouldn't consider it. I don't know what your game is, but your charm won't wash with me. Will you please go, or do I have to put you off?'

'It's all right.' Jay affected to be unperturbed, even though she was disappointed by the sea gypsy's off-hand manner. Seen at close quarters he was more handsome than she had imagined—full, sensuous lips, slightly flared nostrils and dark unfathomable eyes framed in a mahogany face with dark hair curling about his neck and ears.

Had he really been as uninterested as he made out? Most men were attracted by Jay's luxurious black shoulder-length hair and green almond-shaped eyes which flashed fire or humour at their owner's wish. Now they registered chagrin and Jay wondered whether he had been crossed in love, this being the reason for the type of life he now led. 'I'm going,' she concluded. 'All the best on your voyage. When do you sail?'

'As soon as I'm ready,' came the curt reply, head once again bent over his work.

Now, as the boat throbbed across the surface of the water, Jay recalled her abrupt dismissal. He probably had not given her another thought, whereas Jay herself had been unable to dismiss the dark-skinned man from her mind. She had told no one about her proposed experiment today. Her friends would probably say she was mad to allow any man to bother her like this, but it was an emotion she was incapable of controlling, and Rick would have absolutely forbidden her to take out his boat alone. He didn't seem to realise that she was eighteen and perfectly capable of looking after herself.

Jay glanced back towards the shore, half afraid that someone had seen her departure and might even now be racing in pursuit. But all was clear. Land was slowly disappearing from sight. Soon she would be able to stop and maybe discover the secret of the gypsy's love for the sea and his own company in preference to others.

When she was out of sight of all land Jay stopped the engine. The noise died away and the little boat slowed down. The earlier fresh wind had dropped on this late summer day and soon she was bobbing gently on the smooth surface. Apart from the occasional lap of water against the boat's side and a distant cry of seagulls no other sound could be heard. Jay relaxed on the wooden seat, hands behind her head, allowing the all-pervading peace to steal over her. Never before had she felt so free. It would be an idyllic existence—in small doses—but year in and year out? The sea gypsy supposedly had his periods ashore, but he must spend many days, weeks even, with no one but the wind and sea for company. What did he do? How did he pass his time? Didn't he ever feel like taking a crew along? Surely any man, no matter how much he enjoyed solitude, would get tired of this sort of life after a while?

At length Jay prepared to return. No matter how she tried to understand him the sea gypsy would always remain a mystery. The engine started and then petered out. At first Jay felt no alarm, but when after several more attempts still nothing happened a thread of fear wove through her body. Frantically she turned the key again and again. Lifting the engine cover she gazed despairingly at the complex machine. What did she look for? The workings of a motor were an enigma to her.

She slammed back the lid and sat down. What next? There was no other boat in sight; it could be hours before she was spotted. Why had she been so foolish? What madness had driven her out here? A man she didn't understand, would never understand in a million years—and what was more, a man who had no interest in her. It was doubtful she would ever see him again. By the time he had circumnavigated the world she would be several years older and wiser, and probably married—not that she had anyone in mind. The sea gypsy alone filled her thoughts, but as he had made it perfectly clear that she was in his way, and as he had now sailed out of Brixham Harbour, there was no point in dwelling on him.

She searched in vain for something with which to paddle the boat. The need had never arisen before, so she presumed her brother had never thought to equip himself with a pair of oars.

Despondently Jay flopped back on to her seat. In an hour or so it would be dark; there would be no hope at all of anyone finding her then. Her only consolation was that Rick would discover that his boat—and his sister—were missing and send out a search party. All she had to do was wait!

Time passed slowly. Without even a radio to relieve

the monotony Jay soon became fed up with her own company. She wondered again how the sea gypsy could possibly enjoy such a life. Yet he must. Why else would he perpetually return to the sea? She scanned the horizon. Even the sight of his sails would be something, although Jay knew there was not the slightest hope of him seeing her. The motor boat represented but an insignificant spot on the vast surface of the English Channel. Unless someone was deliberately searching for her it was doubtful whether she would be seen.

As the sky darkened so too it began to get colder. Jay shivered and searched the cabin for one of Rick's sweaters, temporarily giving up her watch. She had been afraid to take her eyes off the surrounding water for fear another vessel hove into sight. Was it always so quiet, she mused, or had she been unfortunate in choosing this particular time of day to get stranded? There were no jerseys, but she found an oilskin which she decided would serve the purpose of keeping out the cold.

It had grown even darker in those few minutes and soon Jay was surrounded by total blackness. A few stars blinked down at her and a crescent moon watched lazily from its suspended position in the sky. They did little to alleviate the shadow of night, and after spending another hour's lonely vigil Jay decided to try and get some sleep. There seemed little hope of anyone finding her before morning.

She found tea and sugar and powdered milk in the tiny galley, but no fresh water. It had not occurred to her to check as she had had no intention of staying out

11

for more than a couple of hours. So now, hungry and thirsty, as well as cold and frightened, she could do nothing but curl up on the bunk. Despite her fears Jay was confident she would be rescued in the morning and in a surprisingly short time the rocking motion of the boat soothed her to sleep.

She had no idea that a cutter had appeared as if from nowhere, the light in its rigging a signal for passing ships. The skipper had hove to for the night and Jay was gradually drifting towards him . . .

A jarring sensation woke her as the two vessels met, followed a few seconds later by an angry demanding voice.

'Hey, down there! What the devil are you playing at?'

Jay paused in her action of scrambling from the bunk, every nerve end attuned to the man outside. There was no mistaking his identity. Hadn't he filled her thoughts for the last few hours, to say nothing of the weeks between their last encounter—and now he was here! Not the meeting she had hoped—her thoughts had been of romance, candlelight and roses—all the stuff that dreams are made of.

'Ahoy, there. Is anyone aboard?'

The sea gypsy broke into her reverie and Jay quickly climbed up on deck. The yacht seemed to tower above her, the glow from his lamp defining an angry form looking down.

'I'm sorry,' she called. 'I had no idea——'

He snorted impatiently. 'If you've damaged my topside being sorry won't help. What's the idea, drifting like this?'

He sounded so angry that Jay flinched. 'I—I can't get the engine going. I was tired—I thought I'd——'

'Take a rest and damn everyone else.'

'There was no one about,' protested Jay, feeling he was being unfair. 'I'd been waiting hours to be rescued. You can't blame me for trying to get some sleep.'

'If my boat's damaged I shall. Push yourself away while I throw the fenders over, then I'll come and see what I can do.'

Jay obeyed, waiting with some trepidation as he swung himself easily over the side of *Romany II*. He secured the two boats together with a rope, his bulk dwarfing the motor cruiser and making her realise how little room there was for two people.

At length he turned and shone the torch on her face. From his reaction it was clear that until this moment he had had no idea who she was, and although his expression was hidden his voice told her he was far from pleased by his discovery.

'You!' Disbelief, following accusingly by, 'Is this another of your ruses? I might have known no one in their right senses would deliberately ram another vessel in the middle of the night.'

'As if I would!' objected Jay strongly. 'Credit me with some sense. I know how much pride you take in your yacht.'

'Then you must also know that I never take passengers. Didn't I make myself clear the other day?'

'Perfectly. You really must believe me. I had no idea you were anywhere near. I watched you go this morning and——' She stopped, realising she had given away her interest in him.

'Do go on.' He still flashed the torch and she put up a hand to shield her eyes. It was like a third degree. Why didn't he look at the engine?

'I'm waiting. You watched me go—and then what?'

'Er—nothing. The fact that I decided to take out my brother's boat has nothing to do with you. I thought you would be miles away by now.'

'Ah, so you admit you did think about me?'

Of no one else, to herself, but aloud Jay said, 'I guess everyone knew you'd sailed this morning and thought of you in one way or another. You've got quite a reputation.'

'But not one for abducting pretty girls,' he said drily, 'even if they do invite themselves on board.' Jay was about to hotly deny this statement when he continued, 'Let's take a look at the engine—and if you've tampered with it just to make me think you've broken down I shall know, so be warned.'

Hovering behind as he lifted the engine cover, Jay said, 'You don't have a very good opinion of me. I'm sure I don't know what I've done to deserve such treatment.'

'Little girls who try to plot their way aboard a lonesome sailor's yacht are asking for trouble. Didn't your mother ever tell you not to talk to strangers?'

Jay stiffened. 'I'm old enough to know what I'm doing.'

14

'Old enough maybe, but wise enough—I'm not so sure.' He straightened and faced her. 'Say I had decided to take you on as crew. What do you know about me? How do you know I could be trusted? Or——' his eyebrows lifted mockingly, 'maybe that's what you wanted. Maybe that's the type of girl you are——'

'How dare you!' Jay's hand snaked across his face with a resounding slap. 'How dare you say such a thing!'

Her attack took the sea gypsy by surprise and the torch dropped from his fingers. The lamp in *Romany II*'s rigging cast an eerie glow across his tense body and Jay flinched as he took a step towards her. What have I done? she thought. It was true, she knew little about the man and here she was—alone, at his mercy. If only she had never taken on that stupid bet! She stepped backwards, felt the hard sides of the boat and realised there was no escape. Whether her terror showed she did not know, for suddenly he laughed, a mirthless sound in the still of the night. 'Fear not. I'll do you no harm, though God knows you deserve it.' He probed his cheek gently. 'No one's ever hit me before, least of all a chit of a girl.'

'I'm eighteen,' declared Jay hotly, anger beginning to take the place of fear.

'Girl—woman—what's the difference? You're all the same. By the way, I've found out what your trouble is.'

'You have?' Her temper evaporated and relief took its place. 'Can you help?'

He shook his head. 'Afraid not. It's very serious.'

15

'Oh, no!' Visions of Rick's face floated before her. Of course he would blame it all on her when she got back—*if* she did. She was beginning to have her doubts.

'You've run out of petrol.'

'Is that all?' Jay smiled happily. 'Thank goodness! I thought there was something radically wrong.'

'I can't understand why you never checked it before you set off. No one but a lunatic would do a thing like that.'

'I didn't intend going far. Just a short trip.'

'Even so it would be the obvious thing to do.'

'I realise that now,' rejoined Jay tartly, 'but I didn't check it, so it's no use going on. If you could let me have some petrol I'll willingly pay for it.'

'I wish it were so simple, but I don't carry spare cans for damsels in distress, I'm afraid I can't help.'

'But you must do something.' Jay looked at him imploringly. 'I can't stay here. Can you tow me back?'

'Not a hope. I'm all set for France and nothing or no one will make me turn round.'

He spoke firmly and Jay realised there was little likelihood of persuading him to change his mind. He probably thought that if she was stupid enough to get herself into such a situation she would have to find her own way out. He was a hard man—she should have known better than to ask for help. Even now his eyes glittered in the dim light and she felt sure he was taking pleasure in her distress. 'At least radio to shore for me,' she said at last. 'Get them to send someone out. You can't leave me like this.'

'I have no radio,' came the unexpected reply. 'I like

16

to do things the way our forefathers did.'

Jay felt near despair. Where was the romantic picture she had built of the sea gypsy? *He* would never have left her to fend for herself. He would have rescued her without hesitation. But this man—he was—he was hateful. Surely he could do something?

His next words were as though he had read her thoughts. 'There is one way out of this situation—no, two, if you count waiting in your boat until someone else spots you and comes to your assistance.'

'Which is completely out of the question,' returned Jay sharply. 'How long do you think I'd last without food and water? It might be days before anyone finds me.'

His brows shot up. 'You certainly have got yourself into a load of trouble. That leaves my other suggestion as the only possible alternative.'

'And that is?'

'You come on board with me. We'd have to set this boat adrift, of course. I wouldn't consider towing it.'

Jay stared. 'You mean—go to France—with you?'

'What other choice is there? Besides, isn't it what you wanted?'

'Because I made a mistake it doesn't mean I'll make the same one again.'

'You mean it was a blunder to ask for a trip out with me?'

'Precisely. If I'd known what you were like I would never have entertained the idea.'

'This is interesting.' He folded his arms and looked

at her, head to one side. 'Do go on. No one's ever said anything like this to me before.'

'How fortunate for you! Otherwise you might not have such a high opinion of yourself.'

'How do you know I have that?'

'Your whole attitude. Lord and master of the seas. Is that how you see yourself? Pleasing no one but you and caring not a jot that someone might need your help. And I mean *need* it. Not a put-up job to try and wheedle their way on board.'

'You're very convincing. I almost feel like believing you—if I didn't know better.'

'Oh, go to hell!' Jay stamped her foot and turned her back on him, staring out across the black sea, seeing nothing and wishing devoutly that she had never heard of the sea gypsy, let alone let him get under her skin. To think she had once thought she liked him—despite the fact that he had turned her off his yacht. She should have known then that he had no heart, that women meant little or nothing to him. The trouble was, she needed his help. What choice had she but to accept his offer? None at all. Her only solution was to swallow her pride and agree.

CHAPTER TWO

'SORRY I can't oblige,' returned the sea gypsy. 'Hell's not a place I'd care to visit; but if you're determined I can be of no help I'll go back to bed.'

When Jay turned he was already climbing over the boat's side. 'Wait!' she called. 'I—I will come—but it's my parents. They'll be frantic—isn't there some way we can let them know?'

'You can send a telegram when we get to France.'

'But they don't even know I've taken the boat.'

He snorted. 'Is there no end to your stupidity? In any case there's not much we can do now. Are you coming or not?'

'I suppose so.' Jay watched as he hauled himself back on to *Romany II*, then reluctantly accepted his helping hand. The shock of physical contact caught her unawares and she stepped back immediately her feet touched the deck, unable to understand why she should feel this thrill of pleasure after the way he had treated her.

He cut the little boat adrift and Jay watched until it disappeared from the circle of light. With its going she felt that this was also the severance of her life in England. It was nonsense, she knew, but she couldn't shake off the feeling that something was going to happen. As the sea gypsy had carefully pointed out she knew nothing at all about him and there was no way she could escape should he prove to be an undesirable companion. It was a most unfortunate situation.

She could imagine her mother's reaction when she did not return home. Even now there was probably a search going on. Had Rick missed his boat? What if it was found—empty—before she contacted them from France? Her family would immediately presume she had drowned. Jay buried her face in her hands, unable to bear the thought of her mother's grief.

'Crying won't solve your problem.' The sea gypsy stood close behind her. 'Stop feeling sorry for yourself. Remember, you wanted to crew for me, now's your chance.'

Jay ignored his last remark, partly because she knew nothing at all about sailing and partly because she did not want him to find out—yet. 'It's my parents I'm worried about. They will think I'm——' Her voice broke and she could not finish, but if she expected sympathy there was none forthcoming.

'You have only yourself to blame. You should have thought of these things. Let's go below. I'll make us a hot drink before we bed down for the night—or what's left of it.'

Jay followed him through the hatch and down the steps into the saloon. Here it was warm and comfortable and as he busied himself at the stove she looked about her with interest. The galley was tucked tidily away beside the companion ladder and in the main part of the saloon where Jay stood a settee ran along either side. A sleeping bag was tossed untidily into a heap on one of them where, Jay guessed, the sea gypsy had hurriedly scrambled out after colliding with her boat. A curtain hung across an opening at the other end of the cabin and everywhere paintwork gleamed and fittings sparkled.

Gingerly Jay sat down on the edge of the unused settee. The sea gypsy worked silently and efficiently and within a few minutes handed her a steaming mug. He sat down on the bunk opposite. 'As we're about to be shipboard companions perhaps you'd like to tell me your name?'

'Jay Gordon,' she provided, deliberately avoiding looking at him. He made her feel uncomfortable, a bit like a schoolchild who has been chastised for doing wrong.

'And my name's August,' he returned, 'in case you didn't already know?'

'I've only heard you referred to as the sea gypsy.' Impulsively Jay held out her hand. 'Pleased to meet you, Mr August.'

'Not Mr. Just August,' and he took her hand in his firm brown one. Again Jay felt a thrill of pleasure at his touch. Even his surly attitude could not dispel the physical attraction he held for her. 'The sea gypsy, eh? I like that. It describes exactly how I feel. I've always been an incurable wanderer.'

'Surely you have another name?'

'No—just August.'

'I see. I really am most grateful to you—er—August.

Goodness knows where I'd have finished up if you hadn't happened along.'

'I prefer not to dwell on it. The more I think about your irresponsible behaviour the more annoyed I become. Checking petrol and water is one of the rudiments of boating. Even a child would know that.'

'But——'

He interrupted her rudely. 'I know what you're going to say. You didn't intend going far. That doesn't matter. As you've found out, long or short trip, you need fuel, or at least some other form of propulsion. I'm surprised your brother didn't keep a set of oars on board.'

'He hasn't had the boat long,' defended Jay, 'and I hate to think what he'll say when he finds out that I've lost her.'

'He can claim insurance,' offered August casually, 'and you have two or three days in which to think up an excuse.'

Jay looked at him aghast. 'Two or three? So long? I thought we'd be there tomorrow.'

'Then you'll have to think again. This is no ocean liner. I cruise at my own speed, dependent of course on the weather. If it wasn't for this calm I would be miles away by now, and you—well, who knows what would have happened to you.'

'Looks like I have to thank the weather for saving me, but surely, under these special circumstances, you could use your motor and get me to France a bit quicker? You don't know what my family are like.

They've probably got all the police in Devon searching for me by now.'

'No doubt, but there's nothing I can do.'

'Meaning you won't,' retorted Jay hastily. 'You've gone out of your way to be horrid to me and you intend seeing that I suffer some more. What kind of a man are you?'

'A perfectly reasonable one,' came the smooth reply. 'You really don't listen to anything I say, or if you did you'd realise I have no motor. I sail with the wind.'

Jay stared. 'I don't believe you. You're saying that because you know it will upset me.'

'Take a look for yourself,' invited August, his lips twitching. 'You'll soon see.' He drained his cup and placed it on a locker at the end of the bunk before sprawling lazily back against the padded side of the boat.

Jay looked at him warily. There was something in his voice that told her he was speaking the truth. 'I'll leave it till morning,' she said at last, unwilling to admit that he might be right. 'Thanks for the tea.' She rose and nodded towards the curtain. 'Is that where I'm to sleep?'

'Not tonight,' he replied blandly. 'I'm afraid I hadn't catered for female company. You'll have to make do where you are and tomorrow I'll see what I can sort out.'

'You mean that——' Jay stared at the bunk behind her and then at the one on which August sat a few feet away. 'That—I'm to sleep here—with you?'

He nodded solemnly. 'It's the best I can offer—take it or leave it.'

Jay went hot at the thought of sleeping within arm's

reach of this man. It was unthinkable, yet what option had she?

He picked up their empty cups and squeezed past her into the galley. 'I can't wait while you make up your mind. When I've washed these I'm going to bed. There's a spare sleeping bag in that cupboard.'

Reluctantly she pulled out the bag. Fear prickled her spine, yet when she thought logically there was no more danger sleeping here than behind the curtain. The only difference would be the degree of privacy. If August intended taking advantage of her it would not matter where she slept. She glanced covertly in his direction. He was drying the cups—in a matter of seconds he would be finished. Quickly now, her only thought to undress while his attention was elsewhere, she slipped out of her sweater and trousers and wriggled down between the cool covers. She turned her back on the saloon, but even so was aware of every move the sea gypsy made.

For a few seconds he stood looking down at her 'Glad to see you've come to your senses,' he grunted, then she heard the rustle of clothes as he undressed and folded shirt and trousers before straightening his bag and climbing inside. The light went out. He gave a few indistinguishable noises as he wriggled to find a comfortable position. Subconsciously Jay held her breath, waiting—for what? She did not completely trust this man, but when his breathing at last told her he was asleep the girl relaxed and it was not long before she too slept.

When Jay awoke it took a few seconds to realise that

24

she was not at home in her comfortable bed, but in a strange man's yacht, and judging by the movement of the vessel they were now on their way to the French mainland.

A board had been slotted in at the side of her bunk and as Jay was flung mercilessly against it she was grateful for her companion's solicitude. The weather had changed dramatically. The boat rolled first one way and then the other. Jay peered over the top of the board. The other bunk was empty—all evidence of its occupant gone. She presumed he was on top doing whatever it was he had to do with the sails to keep the yacht going in the right direction.

Removing the board, Jay swung her legs over the side. She felt decidedly queasy and was wondering what the toilet facilities were aboard *Romany II* when August appeared in the companionway.

He took one look at her ashen face and pointed to a door near the curtain which she had not previously noticed.

'I'm one of the lucky ones who don't suffer from seasickness,' commented August, when she returned to the saloon. 'But never mind, it won't last long. You'll feel much better tomorrow.'

Jay grimaced and gratefully accepted the shirt he offered. In her discomfort she had forgotten her state of undress. Even now she felt too ill to be embarrassed and crawled back into her sleeping bag confident she was going to die. If only she had not started on this foolhardy adventure; if only she had never accepted that bet!

'I was hoping you'd take over the cooking,' said August wryly. 'Seems I'm not so lucky. What would you like?'

'Don't mention food,' groaned Jay, 'I couldn't eat a thing,' and when the smell of frying bacon reached her a few minutes later she felt even worse. The final insult came when August pulled out a table next to her bunk and sat down to eat his meal. The motion of the boat seemed not to bother him at all and Jay was sure he was enjoying her discomfiture. Probably thinks it serves me right, she mused. In fact I bet he hoped I'd feel this way as a punishment for causing him so much trouble.

'If this wind keeps up we'll make France in record time,' volunteered August. 'She's running under full sail.'

Jay nibbled one of the biscuits he placed before her. 'I'd sooner it was calm. I can't stand much more of this.'

'You'll soon get your sea-legs. Try not to think about it.'

'It's easy for you to talk,' retorted Jay. 'You don't know what it's like.' Never before had she felt so ill, yet August was behaving as though it was nothing.

'I can imagine, but there's no point in feeling sorry for yourself.'

'I'm not. I feel dreadful. Can't you do something?'

' 'Fraid not. The weather's out of my control, and your sickness—well, you'll have to let that take its course. Pity you didn't prepare yourself. I believe there are all sorts of pills on the market.'

Jay glared. 'As I didn't expect to make such a long trip, and as I've never reacted like this before, I could hardly be expected to take anti-sickness tablets.'

'So you're still sticking to your story? I thought this unpleasantness might induce you to tell the truth.'

Jay closed her eyes. She didn't feel like arguing and at the moment she didn't care what he thought. All she wanted was to be left alone.

She must have slept, for when she next looked around the saloon was empty, though the yacht still rolled and she could hear the sea lashing over her deck and sides. The rest of the day remained a hazy memory. In between bouts of nausea she could recall August's occasional inquiry as to her health, though for the biggest part of the time he remained up on deck. She was only vaguely aware when he bedded down for the night, conscious too that the motion of the boat became less violent. She awoke when the first light of dawn streaked the sky with pale green fingers, conscious that her easier frame of mind was due to the fact that she no longer felt ill.

August still slept. One brown sinewy arm lay loosely across the top of the cover, broad shoulders bared and the back of his head towards her; dark wiry hair curling low into the nape. She watched him for a few seconds trying to guess what his reaction to her indisposition yesterday had been. She recalled the few cross words over breakfast and knew that he had every right to be annoyed. Not only had he been practically forced into giving her a lift, but he had also had to turn nurse as well. Thank goodness she was better now.

She hated the thought of being in his debt for any longer.

Stealthily she pulled her legs out of the sleeping bag, straightening down August's crumpled shirt as she did so. If she was quiet she could get washed and dressed before he stirred.

She pressed her toes to the floor and stood up. But what Jay had not accounted for was her weakened condition. No sooner did she put her full weight on her legs than her knees buckled and she was flung forward across August's bunk.

A startled cry escaped as she found herself practically cheek to cheek with him, her hands resting heavily on his body. Dark eyes, still heavy from sleep, looked up in surprise.

'What's going on?' he asked thickly.

'I—I'm sorry. I fell.' It was as though she had been robbed of all her strength. Jay tried in vain to summon the energy to move.'

'What were you trying to do?'

'Get up, what else?' It was a stupid question. Surely he didn't think she had thrown herself at him on purpose? But his next words made it clear that he had.

'Are you sure you didn't do that deliberately? For the same reason you rammed my boat?'

Jay stiffened. 'And what is that supposed to mean?'

'How you enjoy playing the little innocent,' he remarked. 'You look as though butter wouldn't melt in your mouth, yet you fall all over me and then pretend not to know what it's all about. I wonder how you'd react if I took you up on your invitation?'

From somewhere Jay found the strength to move, but only as far as the edge of the bunk, for with a vice-like grip his fingers caught her arm. He was fully awake now and a gleam of amusement shone in his eyes. 'Would you scream if I tried to kiss you?' he continued. 'Would you struggle if I put my arms about you? Or would you lie back and enjoy it? Isn't that what you want?' Jay was about to hotly deny such thoughts when he answered his own question. 'I wouldn't give you the pleasure. I detest women of your sort.'

'And I hate men who think they know everything,' retorted Jay. 'Doesn't it ever cross your mind that you might be wrong?'

'How else can I interpret your behaviour?' His grip tightened and he shook her none too gently. 'You don't bother to deny my accusations.'

'You're hurting me!' Jay struggled to free herself. 'Please let me go.'

'When you tell me the truth.'

'You wouldn't believe me if I told you.'

'Try me.'

'Why should I? Why should I defend my actions? My conscience is clear and if you were half the man I thought you were you'd believe me.'

August let her go, but as she stumbled back to the opposite settee he sat up and looked at her with renewed interest. 'That's the second time you've admitted to thinking about me. Am I supposed to be flattered by your attention? Our meeting can't be as innocent as you make out, but I won't press it now. You still don't look well. Though I shan't forget—I'll find out sooner or later exactly what's behind that scheming brain of yours.'

His cutting tones hurt Jay. Why was he so harsh? Why did he find such difficulty in believing her? Here was one man who stirred her senses as had no other; yet he treated her as though she was the lowest of the low. He had no respect. He questioned every move she made—always arriving at the wrong, and inevitably the worst, conclusions.

Jay was not normally prone to crying, but in her present weakened state she could feel the prick of tears. Blinking hurriedly, she took refuge behind a spate of angry words. 'You think you're so clever, it doesn't occur to you that people have emotions. You've lived so long alone you've forgotten what it feels like to love —or to hate; to cry or to laugh; to share your feelings with someone else and in return participate in their affections.' She paused for breath before going on, 'I pity you, August. With all my heart I pity you. You have no idea what you're missing.'

His eyes narrowed as he listened to her outburst, but he gave no indication that he was moved by what she said. 'You think I'm incapable of loving,' he uttered at last, so quietly that Jay had to lean forward to hear him. 'But when you've been hurt as much as I have it kills everything inside. All that is left is a body that goes mechanically on—because that's the way life is—and a broken heart that can never be mended. The sea is my love now. She's given me more pleasure than any woman, and if I die at sea at least I shall die happy.'

Without giving her the opportunity to say anything

further August sprang from his bed and pulled on a pair of cotton trousers. He washed in the stainless steel sink in the galley, donned a navy sweater and climbed the stairs. 'It's all yours,' he called over his shoulder, 'if you feel like getting up. I'll be back in ten minutes to cook breakfast.'

'I'll do that,' responded Jay impetuously, feeling all at once sorry for this man. If only she had known ... She was beginning to see more clearly now the reason for his behaviour.

'Not today. Wait until you're properly better.'

Jay realised the sense behind his words when a short while later as August cooked breakfast she experienced again the pangs of nausea.

By lunchtime, however, she felt much better and ventured up on deck. August had left her strictly alone all morning. Whether he regretted his earlier confession she did not know, but whatever it was he seemed intent on keeping himself very much to himself.

A fresh breeze filled their sails and the *Romany II* raced through the water. The bow-wave reached halfway up her deck and Jay felt that he ought to do something to reduce their speed. To her inexperienced eye it did not look safe and she wished she had remained below where none of the aspects of sailing reached her. About to return she was arrested by August calling, 'Don't go. You're feeling better, I see. We might possibly reach France by evening if we keep up our speed.'

She joined him at the helm. 'I never realised yachts moved so quickly.'

'She handles beautifully. I get a thrill every time I

sail her. Can't you feel it?' His black eyes shone as he looked at her, confirming that this was indeed the love of his life.

'I'm not sure that I do,' she said, looking up at the great press of canvas. 'I feel that—that it's running away with itself.'

He looked at her in surprise. 'And you wanted to crew for me? What type of a sailor are you?'

This was the time to confess, to put right the impression that she was accustomed to sailing. Yet still Jay hesitated. August would be angry and she did not want him to berate her again, although she knew now that it was not herself alone that caused his anger. Someone as yet unknown had done this to him and as a result Jay had to suffer. She felt a sudden dislike for the woman who had caused this bitterness. So instead she smiled and said, 'Not quite in this class, but I've no doubt I could manage.'

'Admirable sentiments, though if conditions keep up there'll be no need for you to show me your skill. It's only on very rare occasions when I feel I could do with an extra pair of hands. Even so I've managed perfectly well up till now.'

Relieved that he was not going to invite her to put her supposed crewmanship into action, Jay said, 'How long do you propose staying in France?'

He shrugged. 'A few days perhaps. I have no set schedule. I like to please myself. Have you any particular reason for asking?'

He put the question innocently, yet Jay felt sure he was wondering whether once again she would *force* her attentions on him. 'None at all, except that if I can't get a ferry back straight away I would have nowhere to sleep.'

'I won't see you without a bed,' he said pleasantly. 'I'm not that hard.'

'There is one other thing.' It was a question that had worried Jay for some time but which she had deliberately pushed to the back of her mind. 'I—I have less than a pound with me.'

'Are you asking me to find your fare?'

'I wouldn't dream of it.'

His lips quirked. 'Then what do you propose doing?'

'I'll think of something,' she replied airily. It had been too much to suppose that he might offer to help—and she wouldn't beg.

'There's always the British Consul if you're really stuck. I'm sure *they* wouldn't be able to resist your hard luck story.'

'You mean they'd be more human than you?' stung into retaliation. 'That wouldn't take much doing.' His jaw tightened and for a brief moment Jay wished she hadn't spoken so hastily. Then the moment passed. Why should she feel sorry for him? Most people were hurt at some time or other, but that did not mean they had to dwell on it for the rest of their life. If everyone did that the world would be a sorry place. Why couldn't he forget what this woman had done to him? Time was supposed to be a great healer. How long did he need? 'You're a hard man, August. Can't you see that you are your own worst enemy? You can't judge everyone by— by——'

'My ex-wife?'

Jay flinched at the coldness in his voice. She hadn't realised he'd actually been married to the woman.

'Why not?' he continued. 'I've never met anyone any different.'

'Because you've never given yourself a chance,' she retorted. 'You're too busy tarring everyone with the same brush to stop and look at the person underneath. Wake up, August. Look around. You might be surprised by what you find.'

He stared out to sea almost as if she wasn't there, and Jay watched the arrogant, tanned face. Saw the lines round his eyes caused by constant squinting into the sun, his full lips now drawn into a tight line. Her heart contracted. How could any woman hurt him like this? What was it his wife had done? She must have loved him once—what had happened?

'Would *you*?' he asked suddenly. 'Would *you* risk it again? If so you're made of stronger stuff than me. I've finished with all women. They're the curse of the earth.'

Jay did not know what to say after that. He had made it perfectly clear that he had no intention of changing his outlook. It was futile trying to reform him.

After a few seconds' uncomfortable silence she returned to the saloon. How could you get through to anyone as fixed in their views as August? Couldn't he see that he was wasting his life? The irony was he didn't think that way himself. He was perfectly happy sailing his yacht—for now. But what happened when he got older—or ill? Who would look after him? It was unnatural to want to spend your whole life in solitude—or that was how it seemed to Jay.

August's voice suddenly came down to her. 'Do you feel up to cooking lunch?'

'Yes, of course,' she called. 'What would you like?'

'Surprise me. I've made the decisions for long enough.'

Jay smiled happily. She would show him how indispensable a woman could be. She would serve a meal fit for a king. Who could tell, it might be the first stage in softening him up.

CHAPTER THREE

AUGUST had brought a good supply of fresh vegetables on board and Jay hummed happily as she peeled potatoes and sliced carrots and onions. She opened a tin of stewed steak, and a sultana pudding to follow and then set about lighting the stove.

She had watched August fill the trough with methylated spirit which he then lit before pumping the handle at the bottom. It all looked so easy. She carefully measured the required amount of spirit, found the matches and lit it, then with a certain amount of trepidation worked the pump exactly as she had seen the sea gypsy do. But instead of the smokeless blue flame she expected a smoky yellow one rose into the air and before long the galley began to fill with smoke. Jay coughed and backed away. She had never used a paraffin stove before and did not know what to do. In her consternation she caught the handle of the pan which held the potatoes and sent them flying across the floor.

Hearing the commotion, August poked his head through the hatch. 'What's going—Good grief! Turn the damn thing off.'

Jay looked at him helplessly. 'I don't know how.'

With a muttered expletive he jumped down beside her, kicking the potatoes from underfoot as he did so. In one swift movement he opened the release valve and within seconds the flame had died down.

'I—I'm sorry,' began Jay tentatively.

'Do you spend your life apologising for your blunders?' demanded the sea gypsy harshly. 'If you didn't know how to work the stove why the devil didn't you say so?' A fit of coughing robbed him of further words. 'Come on,' he choked, 'up on top until this lot clears.'

Mutely Jay followed. So much for her good intentions. 'I really am sorry,' she tried again. 'I don't know what I did wrong. I'd seen you light it and thought I was doing the same.'

'How much meths did you put in?'

'I used your measure.'

'Did you let it burn out?'

'Why, no. Should I have done?'

His eyes rolled skywards. 'There's your answer. The burner wasn't hot enough to vaporise the paraffin. I knew I should have done it myself. Why did I ever ask you?'

'I'll know next time,' she said, trying to sound cheerful, 'and I'll clean up the mess once the smoke's gone.' If only he wouldn't look at her with such contempt. Didn't *he* ever do wrong? From the way he spoke it was as though he thought her incapable of doing anything right. The trouble with him was that he wasn't used to other people around. He had lived so long alone that because someone else made a simple mistake—when he had been doing it right for years—he immediately assumed that that person was an idiot.

'You do realise how much work will be involved?' he asked caustically. 'It won't be simply a matter of picking up potatoes and swabbing the floor. The smoke will have drifted into the saloon—there will be smuts everywhere. Are you sure you'll be strong enough to cope, after your indisposition?'

Even if she couldn't Jay did not intend telling him so. She wasn't going to give him another chance to deride her. 'I'll manage. After all, it was my fault, so I can't expect you to clean up after me.'

The effort of wiping down paintwork and mopping the floor almost proved too much. Jay's sickness had left her weakened and by the time she finished the girl felt almost on the verge of collapse. All the time she was working August made no attempt to see how she was getting on. He left her strictly alone and Jay, although thankful, wondered again what sort of a man he was not to offer assistance. He must be aware of how she felt. Was he enjoying the thought of her working herself to a standstill? Did it give him pleasure to see a woman so close to exhaustion that she hardly knew how to stand? This grudge he had against the fair sex was certainly very much in evidence as far as she herself was concerned. Did he treat all women the same, or did he make sure that he made no contact with the female species?

At this point in her thoughts his head appeared. 'You needn't bother to cook a meal now, I'll make do with a sandwich.'

As she had had no intention of trying to light the

stove again Jay looked up from her undignified position on her knees, saying tightly, 'Don't worry, I didn't intend to.'

August's eyes narrowed at this unexpected rejoinder before he disappeared abruptly from view.

Jay shrugged and remained where she was, leaning one shoulder wearily against a locker. How she was to summon the energy to make sandwiches she did not know. Her body felt drained and lifeless, completely incapable of more work. For a further ten minutes she knelt there feeling bitterly opposed to the man at the helm. It would be a relief when they reached France, for it was clear that whatever she did he would find some reason to complain. A pity—for physically he was easily the most attractive man she had ever met, and after having lived with him for the last thirty-six hours it had been imprinted on her more clearly what a perfect specimen of manhood he was. His body held not an ounce of superfluous flesh. Wide, powerful shoulders tapered into a trim waist. He was deeply tanned, yet his skin had not yet attained that weatherbeaten condition of old seamen. His angular face, which looked at times as though it might have been chiselled from granite, was like polished mahogany, the only lines were on his forehead and round his eyes.

At length Jay forced herself to her feet and prepared a plate of sandwiches and pickles. She found lager in the food locker and opened two cans in preference to wrestling with the idiosyncrasies of the stove for the purpose of making tea. August appeared as if by instinct as soon as the food was on the table, making no comment when he saw the glasses of foaming beer.

Jay nibbled at her sandwich, her appetite as yet not fully restored. August on the other hand ate hungrily and did not speak until the plate was empty. Then he leaned back, glass in hand, and looked at her thoughtfully.

'Have you decided what you're going to do when we reach the mainland?'

He sounded as though he was in a hurry to get rid of her, thought Jay unkindly, not that she blamed him. In his eyes she must have appeared clumsy and foolish —not at all the competent sort of person he would wish to crew for him.

'When I telegraph my parents I'll ask them to transfer some money from my bank account. It might mean a short wait, but there's not much else I can do.'

He still studied her. 'I see—and while you're waiting?'

Feeling suddenly very unsure of herself, Jay began. 'You—did say that you wouldn't see me without a bed. I rather hoped that——'

'That was before you created chaos out of a simple job like cooking lunch. If I let you stay on how do I know you won't wreck my home altogether?'

'Thanks for the compliment,' retorted Jay drily. 'It's nice to know you have confidence in me.'

'Have you given me cause to think otherwise?'

Jay glared. 'I've hardly had a chance—but don't worry, I wouldn't stay here now if you begged me. I'll book into a hotel until my money comes.' Was that relief on his face, or was she imagining things? 'I'm only sorry that you've been inconvenienced.'

'Me too, though it's broken the somewhat humdrum first leg of my voyage. It makes a change for me to carry a passenger, albeit a sick one for most of the time.'

Curiosity got the better of Jay and forgetting her anger for a moment she said, 'Haven't you ever considered a crew? Surely it would relieve the monotony when you're at sea for weeks at a time?'

He finished his glass of lager before answering. 'It's a risk I'm not prepared to take.'

Jay frowned. 'What do you mean?' She didn't see how a companion could be a risk.

'If I make a mistake, whether in charting my route or a simple matter like ordering supplies, I have only myself to blame. In point of fact I make darn sure that everything's checked and double checked so that no errors occur——'

'But if you had a man to whom you relegated these duties and anything went wrong, you'd——'

'Be extremely angry,' he finished for her.

Jay shook her head. 'No one's infallible, August, don't you see? Surely everyone's allowed a mistake at some time or other?'

'When it could cost your life?'

'Now you're being dramatic.'

'Not when you stop to think. One error in judgment could mean you end up on a reef with the bottom torn out of your boat. A slip in ordering supplies could mean days at sea without food—or even water.'

'But if you checked everything yourself?' Privately Jay thought he was being over-critical—but that was

41

the type of man he was. Everything had to be done to perfection.

'Precisely. If I did that what would be the point of anyone else coming along? One extra mouth to feed, more supplies to carry, someone else to watch and worry about. No, thank you. I'm a loner and I intend to remain that way.'

Jay wisely kept her own counsel after that. There was no point in a prolonged argument when she knew August would have the last word. He was so accustomed to doing things his way, making all the decisions for himself, that he would not take kindly to the thought that someone else could do the job as well as he.

After she had washed up and put away their plates and glasses Jay lay down on the settee. Her aching limbs told their own story and in a matter of seconds she was asleep. When she awoke the yacht felt unusually still and much colder. She shivered and pulled herself up. It seemed darker all of a sudden and she wondered how long she had slept. Her watch told her that less than two hours had passed—it shouldn't be dusk yet. A glance outside revealed nothing—nothing but a grey blanket of fog!

She climbed the steps to join August. He smiled grimly, beads of moisture hanging from his eyebrows and lashes, a shiny yellow oilskin covering his navy jumper and trousers. He sounded the foghorn and peered ahead into the gloom. Jay could hear the loud sirens of the larger ships and shuddered at the thought of what might happen if they did not see this much smaller vessel beneath their bows. 'Looks like we won't make France today after all,' commented August. 'Why do I always have to run into fog just here?'

'Where are we?' It was impossible to see whether they were in sight of land or not. An occasional shape would loom up beside them, its engines sounding strangely muffled by the heavy fog.

'Outside of Ouessant—the most dangerous part of our crossing. Go back below—there's nothing you can do.'

But Jay frowned and said, 'Ouessant? Where are we heading?'

'Brittany, maybe even Poitou,' with a slight lift of his shoulders. 'I've not made up my mind.'

'But—I thought that——' Jay stopped and looked at him in consternation.

'Yes?' impatiently.

'That you were heading for northern France.' She had surmised he would take the most direct route, never for one moment thinking that he intended making the west coast his destination. She didn't even know if ferries ran from that part of the country or whether she would have to travel across France and pick one up at St Malo or Cherbourg.

'Did I say that?'

'No, but—well, you know how I'm fixed. Surely it wouldn't have been too much trouble to change your plans slightly?'

'I could have done, had I wanted, but I didn't see why I should put myself out.'

His cold indifference angered Jay. Again she was of

the opinion that he was purposely making things difficult for her. 'Perhaps it was asking too much,' she replied aloofly. 'I might have known a man of your type
would never dream of pleasing anyone but himself.'

'Old habits die hard,' was all he said.

Jay turned abruptly and returned to the cabin. As
usual he had had the last word. She shivered and
longed for some warmer clothing. No doubt August
had a supply of thick sweaters, but she wouldn't dream
of asking; not in his present mood anyway. In the end
she decided to have another go at the stove. A mug of
hot soup would help dispel the cold.

This time Jay achieved success. Flushed with
triumph, she bore a steaming mug up to August and
was rewarded by a grateful smile of thanks. 'So you
conquered it after all?'

She nodded. 'Would you like a cooked meal now?
You must be starving.' Her anger had melted and she
felt sorry for him. To be alone at any time was bad
enough, in her opinion, but out here in the fog with
nothing to see except the occasional ghostlike outline
of a steamer—it was like being the only person left in
the world.

'If you think you can avert another disaster, yes.'

His reply was not exactly encouraging, but nevertheless Jay felt sure that this time he would have no
cause for complaint. Indeed the meal was first class and
Jay felt a warm glow of delight when he did it full
justice.

He did not linger once finished, as he feared for the
ship's safety, and long after Jay had settled down for

the night August still sat outside, intermittently sounding his horn and peering out into the gloom. When she expressed a desire to take her turn at the tiller he flatly refused—much to Jay's relief, for she would have known not what to do.

Eventually she slept; fitfully, waking every now and again to see if the weather had improved. August remained on deck for the entire night and when the cold light of dawn replaced the darkness the fog too thinned and eventually dispersed altogether. The sky turned blue and a fresh breeze filled their sails. August set the course and came down below, peeling off his dripping oils and sinking on to his bunk, eyes red-rimmed with tiredness.

'I'll make some breakfast,' offered Jay, who was already washed and dressed, but when she looked round from the galley a few minutes later he had fallen asleep. Smiling softly to herself, she covered him with a blanket and then turning out the stove climbed up on to deck. After their tortuous night it was a perfect morning for sailing. She sat on the foredeck her arms round her knees listening to the slap of the waves against *Romany II*'s hull. Her slim bow appeared to slice through the water as easily as a hot knife through butter. Jay delighted in the feeling of freedom; even the ship seemed to be enjoying herself. It was as though she had been let free after a night in harness and she danced and swayed, lifted and surged, easily and effortlessly.

On this perfect morning Jay began to appreciate some of the pleasures of sailing, understand more fully

August's affinity with the sea. In this, one of her more gentle moods, the great ocean was indeed a lady to be loved—enticing, yet undemanding, elegant in her white crested gown of deepest blue, showing none of her anger that often caused devastation and destruction. Jay tilted her head and looked up at the red sails which pushed the ship forward. They were new, and distinctive—a bit like the man himself. He would stand out in a crowd, not only in stature, though he must be all of six foot four, but as an individual. He was a man of decided opinions and would not hesitate to voice them —whether his listeners would be in agreeance was another matter, but August himself would air his views without fear of being disliked. He would not care. Jay doubted if it would bother him if he had no friends. In fact, it was a debatable point whether he had any.

Jay wondered what type of person would get on well with the sea gypsy. Certainly not anyone of a similar disposition, or one who was easily ruffled. They would need to be able to submit to authority, yet not be too easily swayed, as August would have no time for anyone without a mind of their own. It would take a person of remarkable insight, tremendous patience, and naturally a similar love of the sea to chum up with August— if indeed he allowed anyone to get near him again.

Not surprisingly Jay pondered on the woman who had been his wife. What was it she had done to cause August such pain, such everlasting bitterness that it seemed unlikely he would ever love again? It was not a question she could ask, and as they would be in France within a matter of hours it was doubtful whether the opportunity for him to tell her would present itself. But it was a question that intrigued her. He must have loved his wife once—how could love change to hatred? Jay believed marriage to be a permanent institution and no one should take a partner unless he or she believed it would be a lasting union. So what had happened to upset August's marriage?

'Where's that food you promised me?' August's voice directly behind made her turn with a start. His rope-soled shoes had made no sound on the deck and she was amazed to see him standing so close.

'I'll do it now,' jumping up. 'When you fell asleep I decided that would do you more good.'

Surprisingly he touched her arm. 'Stay a while. I've been watching you and wondered what it was that held your thoughts so deeply.'

They sat together, shoulders almost touching, and looked out across the sparkling, prancing waves. Jay knew he awaited her reply, but how could she tell him that he alone had held her attention? That it was his affairs that interested her. She could imagine his reaction. The hardening of those coal black eyes, the tightening of his lips. 'What I do is no business of yours,' he would say. 'The past is over and forgotten and I don't want to be reminded of it.' But she could tell him how much she was enjoying this morning's ride—and proceeded to do so.

He smiled as she spoke. White teeth gleaming in his tanned face; eyes softening and for once looking kindly at her. 'This is only half the enjoyment. You've never felt the satisfaction of having fought with a storm—

and won; of dicing with death and coming through laughing. Not at the time, I'll grant you, but afterwards you feel ten foot tall and proud of yourself. It's the achievement; the self-satisfaction that wins every time. I'd never change my way of life.'

'Would you marry again?'

Jay knew it was the wrong thing to have asked almost before she had finished, but there was just a chance—a slim one—that he might not resent her question.

The odds were against her, however. His smile faded, to be replaced by a frown. 'No chance. Only a fool makes the same mistake twice.'

'I'm sorry——' began Jay tentatively, wondering if now would be the right time to ask what had happened.

'Spare the pity,' came the cutting rejoinder. 'I don't need sympathy, least of all a woman's. But I do need a good, strong cup of tea.'

In other words, thought Jay as she pushed herself up, you don't want to talk about it. Not that she had really expected him to—but it would help if she knew; how could she ever expect to understand his strange reasoning otherwise?

It was shortly after breakfast when she heard August shout, 'Land ahead!'

A surge of excitement welled within her and Jay scrambled up the companionway to join him. Sure enough there was land—a mere blue shadow at this distance, but France all the same. Soon now she would be able to relieve her parents' anxiety; a problem that had worried her constantly since the onset of the voyage.

They watched together as the blue grey turned to green and eventually into rich woodland with the occasional roof of a chateau showing through the trees. She admired August's expert handling of *Romany II* as they sailed into the Odet estuary and then into the harbour at Bénodet on the Brittany coast.

Once the formalities were over Jay was impatient to find the post office.

'I'll come with you,' offered August lazily, 'in case you should get into difficulties.' There was a twinkle in his eye as he spoke, but Jay failed to see it and bristled defensively, though she deemed it wise to say nothing. It was quite possible that she would need his help in some way or another before the day was over, so it wouldn't do to get on the wrong side of him at the moment.

They found the *bureau de poste* and after several attempts Jay wrote, *Am safe in France. Rick's engine failed. Rescued by sea gypsy. Need money for ferry. Please transfer from my account to bank at Bénodet.*

August, watching over her shoulder, said, 'You seem sure your parents will know who you mean by "sea gypsy"?'

'But of course. Everyone calls you that. They'll know now that I'm in safe company.'

A lift of one mobile brow. 'I'm not so sure. They might think I've kidnapped you.'

'I doubt it. I've heard you described as a lonely man, but never a crooked one.'

'If I've such a good reputation wouldn't it be natural

49

for your parents to assume that I'd loan you the money to get home?'

Jay shrugged. 'Perhaps, but what else can I say?'

'Here, let me write it,' and before Jay had time to object August scribbled a few words on the appropriate form and passed it to the girl behind the counter.

'What have you put?' Jay wished he had shown her.

'Just that you're safe and need money,' he said lightly, and led the way outside.

Had Jay known the truth at that stage she would not have felt so easy in her mind, but now she stood on the pavement blissfully ignorant of the course of events that were about to alter her whole life. 'I suppose the next thing is to find myself a hotel,' she said, looking about her. 'Can you recommend one?'

'I believe the Kastell Moor has a good reputation, especially with British visitors, but——'

He hesitated and Jay looked inquiringly at him, 'It's very expensive, is that it?'

'No, no, I—I've had second thoughts. You can stay on *Romany II*—if you still want to?'

This was so completely in variance with his former attitude that Jay could only stare. What had happened to make him change his mind?

'You'd rather not?' he asked at last. 'I suppose it's natural after the way I've acted. I just thought it would help, that's all.'

'But why?' Jay insisted. 'Why offer now, when you were so firmly against it?'

'Call it my conscience,' he said with a shrug. 'I didn't know I had one till now.' Suddenly he looked ashamed and Jay realised how much it had cost to make this offer.

'I'd love to,' she accepted quickly, flashing him a dazzling smile. 'I didn't really fancy a hotel—not on my own.'

There was no answering smile on August's face. It was almost as though he regretted his burst of generosity. 'Come along, then,' he said, 'you can help me clear out the forecastle. You'll get more privacy sleeping in there.'

Jay was about to declare that she did not wish to put him to any more trouble when she realised he was right. When she was seasick she had felt far too ill to care where she slept, but now it would be different. Although she knew instinctively that he was to be trusted; that he would never take advantage of their being together; the curtain between would put an aura of respectability over their relationship.

The fact that he had relented enough to allow her to sleep aboard proved to Jay that the softening up process had started. August had kept himself to himself for so long that he was in danger of becoming a recluse, an eccentric. It was a pity that in a few days she would be gone. Jay was sure that given time she would be able to change August's outlook; persuade him that all women were not the same, least of all this one who was already more than half way towards falling in love with the man they called the sea gypsy.

CHAPTER FOUR

On the second day of their stay in Brittany Jay watched another yacht glide into the harbour and anchor alongside. She thought no more about it until August, who had been below at the time, came up on deck and began to wave vigorously.

'Ahoy there, Jeff, nice to see you again.'

The ginger-bearded giant of a man looked across, a wide grin splitting his face, 'August! This is great. I never expected to see you.' He looked over his shoulder. 'Hey, Charlie, come and see who's here!'

Jay was astounded when a girl emerged through the hatch. The name had immediately conjured up another man, but this girl was anything but masculine. Shoulder-length blonde hair swung about her shoulders. She wore close-fitting white jeans and a bright red shirt, making Jay even more conscious of the clothes she had worn for the last few days. She had managed to wash out her underwear, but there was no hope of drying out her jumper and slacks overnight, so she had been forced to pull them on again each morning.

'August!' The blonde also appeared, delighted. 'Come on over, I'll make some tea. Bring your friend.'

She looked directly at Jay as she spoke, starting visibly when she saw that his companion was a girl—no doubt, thought Jay grimly, aware of his aversion to women.

The fact that these people were old and apparently favoured friends puzzled Jay too. It did not add up with her impression of August as a lonesome man.

Once on board the *Darling*, as the ketch was called, and after introductions had been made, Charlie invited Jay below to help with the tea, while the two men remained on deck. They had much news to catch up on.

'I'm intrigued,' began Charlie immediately they were out of earshot. 'You must forgive me, but what are you doing with August?'

Jay laughed delightedly. 'You make it sound as though I'm leading him astray!'

'No chance of that,' replied the blonde, 'the man's a woman-hater, in case you didn't know—or at least he was the last time we met.'

'And still is.'

'Then how come you're——' she spread her hands expressively, *'you're together?* I know I must seem rude, but I can't get over it.'

Again Jay laughed, to be interrupted by Jeff poking his head through the hatch. 'What's going on? Can't we all share the joke?'

'Be off with you,' smiled his wife. 'This is woman talk.'

'Well, don't let it hold up the tea. August and I are parched.'

'Tell me when you're not,' she scoffed goodnaturedly, and Jay envied their easy relationship. If only August would treat her in this manner, it would make life so much pleasanter. She had thought, when he had invited her to stay on *Romany II*, that things might be different between them, but he had in fact practically ignored her. She had cooked their meals, feeling it was the least she could do in return for his hospitality, but for the rest of the day August had either disappeared or spent his time messing about with the boat. Jay wondered whether he regretted his decision, but it was a delicate subject and one she felt best left alone.

It was a relief now to have someone to talk to; someone who would understand how she felt, perhaps even sympathise. But where should she start?

'Come on, give,' encouraged Charlie, who had filled the kettle and was now arranging cups and saucers on a tray. 'How did you meet?'

Jay's lips twitched. 'You could say that we bumped into each other, or on the other hand, that he picked me up.'

Charlie's fine brows rose sceptically. 'That doesn't sound like August. Sure you're not kidding?'

'Not at all,' laughed Jay, then more seriously, 'I'd run out of petrol in my brother's boat and accidentally drifted into the *Romany II*.'

'Oh! I can imagine his reaction. What did he say?'

'What didn't he say would be better! I don't think I need tell you. Anyway, it ended up with him offering me a lift, but as he refused to take me back to England he brought me here.'

Charlie was delighted by Jay's confession. 'This is a turn-up for the book. Wait till I tell Jeff! He'll never believe it. But—if I might ask another personal question—why are you still here?'

Jay pulled a wry face. 'I have no money. I've arranged for some to be transferred, but while I'm waiting—I'm—er—living with August.'

'It's incredible.' Charlie shook her head, looking bewildered. 'If you hadn't told me yourself I'd never have believed it—not of August. After what Kate did to him I never thought he'd speak to another woman. It's different with me, he treats me more like a sister than anything else.'

'What happened between August and—er—Kate?' Jay hoped that now she would discover the true facts.

'He hasn't told you?'

'Only that she let him down badly.'

'Then I'm sorry, it's not up to me. If he'd wanted you to know he'd have told you himself. Perhaps he will one day, who knows?'

'I doubt it,' said Jay sadly. 'I shan't be here that long.'

Charlie looked at the dark girl with interest. 'You sound as though you don't want to leave. I can't imagine he's treated you so well. He's been a difficult man to get on with since—well, since the Kate affair.'

'Did you know her?'

'She was my best friend. We grew up together, Kate, August and me. I never thought she'd turn out like that.' She stared into space for a few seconds before shrugging and forcing a smile. 'The men will wonder what's happening. You go up and I'll follow.'

Conversation stopped as Jay approached, leaving

55

the impression that they had been discussing her. As she herself was guilty of the same offence Jay smiled inwardly, lowering herself on to a canvas chair that had been placed at her disposal.

'I hear you've got yourself into a spot of trouble?' Jeff's smile was full of friendly interest.

'You could say that,' acknowledged Jay, wondering exactly how much August had told him. 'I shudder to think what would have happened if August hadn't found me.'

The sea gypsy gave a dry laugh. 'I like that! You know damn well that if you hadn't deliberately rammed me I'd never have spotted you.'

Jay strove to keep her temper, wishing he wouldn't speak in such a way in front of his friends. 'That's your theory, but the truth is, Jeff, we were both asleep at the time. Our meeting was perfectly accidental, though I can't make August believe me. Perhaps you could persuade him?'

The bearded man held up his hand in mock horror. 'Keep me out of it. If you knew August as well as I do you'd know that once he's got an idea fixed into his head nothing will change it. Isn't that right, my friend?'

August inclined his head. 'I've never had reason to believe otherwise. Ah, here's my girl,' as Charlie appeared with the teas. 'Come and sit here and tell me what you've been doing with yourself since I last saw you. How long's it been? A couple of years at least.'

Charlie grinned affectionately and after handing round the teas dropped into the vacant chair beside August. They were soon deep in conversation and Jay marvelled at the change in the man. To see the two of them together you would never believe that he had an aversion to women. Jay felt a pang of jealousy. Why couldn't he talk to her like that? Why did he always treat her as though she was a nobody, a nuisance that he had picked up and would be glad to drop?

Jeff must have guessed something of her feelings, for he patted her arm comfortingly. 'Tell me about yourself. I don't really believe you forced your way on board. What happened?'

As Jay proceeded to relate the course of events that led up to her meeting with the sea gypsy she began to realise that in Charlie and Jeff she had allies. They at least believed her. The trouble with August was that he did not want to. The thought of admitting that he might be wrong was abhorrent.

'No doubt Charlie's told you something about August,' said Jeff. 'You must make allowances. He's had a hard time. It isn't easy for him to relax these days. I must admit when I first saw you with him I thought to myself, "Good old August, got himself a girl at last." But I see now that it's not like that. Pity, you could be good for him. Mind you, the fact that he's let you stay on board is something.'

Jay pulled a face. 'He didn't really want to, but then again he didn't like the idea of my parents getting a bad impression of him if he turned me loose in a strange country.'

'You surprise me.' Jeff's bushy red brows rose dramatically. 'The old August wouldn't give a damn what anyone thought. He's changing, and it must be because of you—there's no other reason so far as I can see.'

'All I can say,' replied Jay, 'is that if he's different now thank goodness I didn't meet him earlier. A more difficult man I've never met.'

She did not realise her voice had risen, nor that Charlie and the sea gypsy had finished their conversation and heard every word of her last sentence.

August looked directly at her, his eyes glinting in their customary cold manner. 'Perhaps I could add to that. You, my little friend, are the most troublesome woman *I* have ever met.' He looked at the other two, who were watching with interest. 'Not only did she nearly hole my ship; she was seasick for two days and when finally she attempted to make herself useful she smoked out the galley.'

Charlie chuckled. 'The trouble with you, August, is that you expect too much.'

'I like that!' he bristled. 'I don't suppose she told you that only a few weeks ago she had the nerve to ask whether she could crew for me?'

'You could do worse,' put in Jeff, his seemingly irrepressible smile still very much in evidence. 'She's a nice little thing. I like her.'

Jay glared round at the company. 'And I prefer not to be discussed as though I weren't here.'

'I'm intrigued,' Charlie smiled. 'Did you really ask him that?'

Jay nodded. 'Though I suppose now is as good a time as any to tell you the truth.' She looked at August as she spoke, cringing inwardly at the accusing look on his face, but nevertheless determined to carry on. 'It was a joke, really. Some of my friends made a bet—that I couldn't get a ride on your yacht.' She swallowed painfully and glanced down at her hands clenched tightly together.

August pounced delightedly. 'I knew it! What did I say? I knew all the time you had it planned. More fool me for offering to help.'

'I don't think that's exactly what Jay means,' interrupted Charlie quietly.

'What else can she mean?' he jeered.

'That the first time I asked you,' put in Jay firmly, 'was because of the bet. Needless to say I lost. But out at sea—I never intended that. Heaven forbid I should be so stupid.'

Silence fell. Clearly they all believed her, except for one man—and it looked as though even he might be having second thoughts.

Suddenly he smiled, though to Jay's watchful eyes it was not a pleasant smile, rather a menacing one. What indignity was he cooking up now?

'How would you like to win your bet?'

She stared. They all stared. Had they heard correctly?

'Well, what do you say?'

Jay shook her head. 'I—er—I don't know what to say. If you mean what I think you mean, I—I'm not sure.'

'Take him up on it,' urged Charlie. 'You won't get a second chance.'

'True,' echoed her husband. 'I'm sure you won't

regret it. There's nothing quite like a life at sea.'

But Jay was not so easily swayed. 'Why?' she demanded. 'You made it perfectly clear a short while ago that you couldn't wait to get rid of me—and I know you've considered me a nuisance ever since that first day.' Besides, there was a vast difference between a short trip—which was what she had envisaged in order to win the bet, and which she had now undertaken— and a trip round the world. It wasn't as if she knew anything about sailing—not that August was aware of this. And her parents—what would they think? How long would she be away? A year? Two? Maybe even three?

It was unthinkable, yet at the same time the challenge sent a shiver of excitement down her spine. It would give her chance to get to know the sea gypsy better. Who could tell—by the end of the voyage he might have got over his antipathy. He might even fall in love with her! Or did his invitation hold some ulterior motive? Did he want to gloat over her inadequacy? Treat her as a slave and pay her back for all the trouble she had caused? It was difficult to know what reason lay behind his offer, but she was quite sure that he had not done it out of kindness, or because he needed a crew.

August was studying her now, openly amused. 'Let's say my appetite's been whetted. I've had a taste of what it's like to have a woman on board, and strange person that I am, I've a fancy for more. If you're worried about your virtue, forget it. There'll be nothing more than a platonic friendship between us. It's the novelty that tempts me. As you know, I've always travelled alone—never had a yen for company, till now. Well, what's your answer to be? A straight yes or no is all I need.'

All eyes were on Jay. She shifted uncomfortably in her seat. She wanted to say yes, but there were so many doubts in her mind. Would it work? If she found life unbearable where could she go? In the small confines of *Romany II* there would be no escape. She would be virtually a prisoner—of her own making, but a prisoner all the same. She would be at the sea gypsy's mercy.

Judging by Charlie and Jeff's expressions they were all for it, and they knew August better than she—and so, against her better judgement, Jay nodded, 'I'll come,' adding quickly, 'though what my parents will say I dread to think!'

Their hosts looked at each other and smiled in agreement. August too was smiling and he said, 'They already know.'

Again Jay was profoundly shocked. 'What do you mean?'

'That telegram,' he replied airily. 'I told them you were coming with me.'

'You did *what*?' Jay's eyes narrowed and she pushed herself up from her seat.

'I said you were circumnavigating the world with me.'

Jay passed a hand across her brow. 'I don't believe you. You didn't think of it until just now—and besides, you didn't know I would agree.'

'I know you better than you think,' he said. 'Wait and see. You should have their reply any time now.'

It was clear he meant what he said and Jay sank slowly down again. 'They'll think I've gone mad. It's not as if they know you,' and then more strongly, 'They won't allow it. They'll come and fetch me back.'

'In that case, if you thought they'd be so set against your accompanying me, why did you agree?'

It was a logical enough question, but one which Jay was not prepared to answer—not truthfully at any rate. She could imagine his reaction if she said she loved him. So instead she parried with another question. 'If you hate women why did you ask me?'

His answer was prompt. 'Because you're different. You haven't tried to make me aware of you as a woman, though I must confess I had my doubts at first. In fact, I think, with training, you'll make a good crew.'

Jay's conscience smote her at these approving words. She really ought to tell him that she knew nothing about sailing. It was hardly likely that he would take along someone who would be more of a liability than an asset. She would do her best, naturally, but, ignoramus as she was, there would undoubtedly be occasions when her inadequacy would trigger off the sea gypsy's anger and impatience.

'I guess this calls for a celebration.' Charlie jumped up. 'It will only be dinner wine, I'm afraid,' and she disappeared below.

The moment had passed. Jay's confession still unmade. As she looked at August as he lumbered after Charlie Jay's heart skipped a beat. Already she knew every line of that proud, angular face, every curve of his muscular body, and was glad she had not spoken. It would break her heart to be parted from him now, though she knew he must never guess at her feelings. Charlie had conjectured, but then a woman is always more intuitive in these things than a man.

Even now she was aware of Jeff observing her keenly and with a supreme effort she pulled herself together. 'It should be fun,' she said lightly. 'I'm quite looking forward to it.'

Jeff pulled down the corners of his mouth. 'Sailing's not all pleasure—there are times when you wish for nothing else but dry land beneath your feet, times when you think the end is near—but I expect you know all about that; you wouldn't have offered to crew otherwise. Done much sailing, have you?'

With a casual shrug Jay said, 'Not as much as you, of course, but—ah, here's the wine,' grateful for the timely intervention which put an end to what could have been a difficult conversation.

The next hour passed swiftly and Jay saw another side to August's character. She found him positively human, laughing and joking in a way she had thought him incapable of. The embittered man had disappeared, though he was still a shade reserved in his manner towards Jay. Nevertheless she was content to sit back and listen. The conversation invariably centred on the sea and ships; of past and future voyages; of hopes and desires; disappointments and losses.

And then Jeff suggested they dine out in one of Bénodet's restaurants. 'It's not often we meet up like this,' he said. 'Let's make it an occasion to remember.'

Because she knew that he was a man who shied away

from company Jay thought August would refuse, and was surprised when he nodded emphatically. 'Good idea. Why didn't I think of it? Jay?'

He looked expectantly across at his new crew member, but the girl shook her head. 'Count me out. I—I don't like eating out.' A lie, but how could she go dressed like this?

August frowned. 'I've no time for silly remarks like that. You're coming.'

'Hang on.' Charlie put her hand on August's shoulder. 'I think I know what's wrong.' She looked across at Jay. 'You have nothing to wear. Is that it?'

Jay nodded miserably.

'Then why the hell didn't you say so?' grumbled August. 'Maybe it's my fault. Perhaps I should have realised, but I've more things on my mind than women's clothes. Why didn't you speak up?'

Not wishing to tell him that he was not exactly the world's most approachable man, and that after her first advances for help had met with opposition she had not felt like asking for further assistance, Jay replied, 'I thought I could manage, at least until my money came. I didn't realise I'd be invited to eat out.'

'Never mind,' put in Charlie cheerfully, 'we're much of a size. You can borrow something of mine.'

'Indeed she will not!' August glared angrily at the two girls and pulled a wad of notes from his hip pocket. 'Here, get what you want. And while you're about it you might as well rig yourself up for the voyage, oilskins and so forth. Charlie will tell you what you need.'

64

'But——' Jay hesitated, 'it will cost a fortune. I can't let you——'

'Pay me back if you like,' he interposed tersely, 'if it will make you feel any better, but I can assure you it's not necessary.'

The girls lost no time after that in taking the dinghy ashore and searching the shops for Jay's new wardrobe. It was impossible to restrain her excitement in buying so many beautiful new clothes, although the cost did worry her somewhat. Everything was so expensive compared to English prices, but Charlie assured her that August could afford it. 'He's a wealthy man, in case you didn't know.'

'I don't see how,' frowned Jay. 'He never seems to work.'

Charlie laughed. 'Don't you believe it! He owns a charter company in the East Indies and thinks nothing of helping out when the occasion demands. Of course the company's grown so big now that he's rarely needed, but at one time he used to do all the work himself. That's how he started.'

Yet something else Jay had learned about August! Today was certainly full of surprises. 'Was he married then?'

A shadow crossed the blonde girl's face. 'No, but it was the beginning of the end. Kate and August had always been friends, but no more. She'd never shown any interest in him as a man, if you know what I mean?'

Jay nodded, reluctant to interrupt what could be a revealing speech.

'When the money began to roll in and it changed

from a one-man concern to a profitable business Kate began to dig in her claws. Of course, neither of us saw it at the time. August was happy—and I was happy that my two best friends had apparently discovered new feelings for each other. I myself had met Jeff by then and was ready to recommend falling in love to anyone. Anyway, they got married and everything was fine for a while. It was when she wanted him to stay at home the trouble began.'

Suddenly Charlie stopped, realising that she had said too much. 'I shouldn't have told you all this. August doesn't like his affairs discussed. He sometimes feels that it's all his fault; that if he'd given in his marriage might have been saved. But I don't think so. I reckon Kate would have left him one day anyway.' She glanced at her watch. 'Gosh, we'd better get back or we'll both be in trouble—and Jay, not a word about what I've told you.'

CHAPTER FIVE

Jay dressed with care for her evening out, pleasurable anticipation adding a sparkle to her eyes and a touch of colour to her normally pale cheeks. Arriving back on *Romany II* after their shopping expedition Jay had found August already washed and changed. It was the first time she had seen him in anything other than his usual seafaring garb and she had been unable to hold back a cry of surprise. The dark, handsome man in a silver grey suit and crisp white shirt looked nothing like her sailing companion of the last few days.

'Is anything the matter?' he asked testily. 'I was beginning to think you'd got lost.'

'N—no. You look different, that's all,' and more devastatingly attractive than ever, she added mentally.

'I'm not entirely uncivilised, despite what you may think. Look sharp now and get ready, I don't like being kept waiting. You managed to get everything?' looking doubtfully at the paper carrier in her hand.

'Oh, yes, they're being delivered tomorrow. I've only brought what I need for now.'

'I see.'

He made his way up the companionway and Jay stared after him, wondering what had happened to his earlier good humour. Then she shrugged philosophically and began to empty her bag. If the man chose to be moody it was nothing to do with her; she intended enjoying their evening out. It might be a long time before such an opportunity came her way again.

Now, as she put the finishing touches to her hair, Jay could not help but observe her heightened colour; but what the tiny mirror in the saloon did not tell her was how appealing she looked in the scoop-necked yellow cotton dress that Charlie had declared would double as a sun-dress in the tropics. Its delicate colour suited her dark hair and honey-gold tan and the full skirt swished about her thighs as she climbed the steps to join August.

It was a relief to be out of trousers and her feet were light as she crossed the deck. August had his back to her, but turned as she approached. Jay's smile faded when she saw his scowl. What was wrong now?

'Wasn't I quick enough?'

'It's not that.' He shook his head as if dazed—and then suddenly smiled. 'You look different, that's all.'

'Touché.' Her smile matched his. 'I trust you approve?'

'I'm not sure,' still looking her up and down.

Jay went hot under his scrutiny.

'Surely you didn't prefer me in scruffy jeans?'

'You looked less like a woman.'

'Oh, I see.' She paused. 'Will it make any difference?'

His brows lifted. 'Not unless you plan it that way.'

Jay bristled. Why did he always think the worst? 'I wouldn't dream of it, but if you want to back down, it's all right with me. Perhaps it wasn't such a good idea. If we're going to be at daggers drawn for the whole journey it's not going to be much fun.'

August shrugged. 'The ball's in your court. If you play the game fairly I can't see anything going wrong.'

'And what are your rules?'

'Now you're being childish.' The frown once again settled on his forehead. 'Come on, let's go before I lose patience altogether.'

In the relaxed atmosphere of the French restaurant and in the company of Charlie and Jeff, Jay was able to forget her disagreement. This time her new job was toasted in champagne. Jay had never tasted the sparkling liquid before and did not realise how potent the drink was. She felt gay and relaxed and although the room sometimes appeared to be circling round her head she continued to eat and drink while maintaining a witty conversation. It was not until Charlie suggested they visit the powder room and she tried to stand that she realised something was wrong.

Charlie, who had noticed for some time that Jay was drinking more than she ought, grabbed her arm firmly and led her away from the table. 'For Pete's sake don't let August see you like this,' she hissed. 'He abominates women who drink too much.'

'I—I'm not drunk,' Jay protested. 'I feel a little lightheaded, that's all. It must be the champagne.'

Charlie smiled and said nothing more until they were safely in the ladies' cloakroom. 'Wash your face in cold water,' she ordered. 'I'll try and get some black coffee without arousing suspicion. I reckon you'll be all right in a few minutes, but if you'd gone on drinking at that rate I hate to think what the consequences would have been.'

When Charlie returned with the coffee Jay was looking apologetic and feeling ashamed of herself. 'I hope I'm not a nuisance,' she said.

'Not to me,' assured her friend, 'but August won't think so if he finds out. Here, sip this. Kate used to drink, especially when August was away. That's why I don't want him to see you like this.'

'Meaning my job will be axed before I start?'

'Afraid so,' nodded Charlie. 'And it would be such a pity. I've a feeling you're going to do him a lot of good.'

'I wish I had your confidence. So far we've done nothing but argue. I still can't think why he's asked me.'

'It is surprising, I must admit.' confessed Charlie, 'especially the fact that he's already told your parents. Had you no idea?'

'None at all, though I wondered why he didn't show me the telegram. What do you think made him do it?'

'It could be'—said Charlie slowly—'that he's beginning to change his mind about women. I think he likes you—more than just a little.'

Jay laughed mirthlessly, the coffee already beginning to have a steadying effect. 'He has a funny way of showing it. I can't weigh him up.'

'I shouldn't try. Be satisfied that he's taking an interest. Isn't it what you want?'

'I suppose so,' Jay admitted, knowing it would be

useless trying to deny anything. Charlie had already intimated an awareness of her reaction towards this unusual man. 'But for heaven's sake, don't tell him.'

'As if I would!' scoffed the blonde. 'We both know that he'd soon change his mind if he guessed how you felt. Don't worry, I'm on your side. I'd like nothing better than to see August a happy man once again. He's spent far too much time brooding these last few years. How are you feeling?'

'Better, I think.' Jay attempted to stand, but sat down again quickly. 'Ooh, my head! Can we wait a bit longer, do you think?' The room was still going round and she was not sure that she could make it back to their table without revealing her condition.

'A couple of minutes, perhaps. We don't want them getting suspicious.'

But even as she spoke there was a discreet tap on the door before it opened and August's frowning face appeared. 'What are you two playing at? Is anything the matter?' and then looking at the empty cup in Jay's hand, 'I thought I saw Charlie sneak past with that—are you ill?'

Jay shook her head and in a desperate attempt to assure him that there was nothing wrong rose swiftly to her feet, fighting the feeling of nausea that suddenly assailed her. 'Why should there be? I'm fine— Oh dear, I think I'm going to be sick,' and she ran from the room.

Immediately afterwards Jay felt much better, but was loth to face August. If he vented his anger on her now she would be unable to contain her tears—and where would that get her? But there was no use putting off the evil moment any longer. If she didn't go out soon he would be after her.

To her relief the outer room was empty. With a hand that shook she combed her hair and applied fresh lipstick, then taking a deep breath braced herself and left the room.

Charlie and August were talking outside. August laughing over some remark made by the blonde girl, but Jay fully expected the smile to disappear when he saw her. It was a pleasant surprise when he held out his hand and with an amused quirk of his brows said, 'Are you feeling better? I didn't realise you'd never tried champagne or I'd have told you to go easy. It can be very potent stuff when you're not used to it. Would you like to go back to the yacht?'

Jay shook her head emphatically, August's unexpected reaction making her feel suddenly so much better. 'Oh, no, I wouldn't dream of spoiling your evening. I'm better now, really I am. I—I'm sorry if I've—made a fool of myself.'

He still held her hand and to Jay's further amazement pulled her closer to him and slid an arm about her shoulders. 'Little idiot,' he murmured. 'But I won't hold it against you—not this time. You weren't to know.' And with his arm remaining round her he led her back to the table.

Jeff was looking about him with a neglected air. 'Ah, here you are! I was about to send out a search party.' He glanced questioningly at Jay and August but passed no comment, merely continuing, 'It's my turn to buy the drinks. What will it be?' displaying extreme offence when everyone laughed.

Far from spoil their relationship as Jay had feared the episode seemed to strengthen August's feelings. He developed a protective instinct, watching over her carefully for the rest of the evening and tucking her arm into his as they made their way back to the ships afterwards.

The girls were unable to speak privately before they parted, but Charlie gave Jay a discreet wink which seemed to say, 'Keep up the good work. You're doing all right!'

Inside the saloon August still retained his mellow mood and the effects of the champagne had disappeared sufficiently to leave Jay feeling warmly happy.

'Let's have a nightcap,' suggested August, producing a key and unlocking a cabinet that up till now had remained closed.

'I don't think I dare,' looking doubtfully at the several bottles huddled together in their cramped quarters. 'Not after——'

'What I'm going to suggest won't hurt you,' he smiled. 'It might help you sleep—nothing more,' and he proceeded to pour golden liquid into a glass taken from special racks in the cupboard door.

'To a pleasant voyage.' He lifted his drink ceremoniously and sank down on the seat beside her.

He seemed different tonight and Jay found herself responding automatically to his mood. He had taken off his jacket and tie and loosened the collar of his shirt. Looking at him, with his sleeves rolled up, hair slightly awry and a warm glint in his eyes that was not normally there, Jay was filled with a wild desire to feel his arms about her waist and his lips on hers. Of course this could never be, for hadn't he said that theirs was to be a strictly platonic association? So, swallowing the constricting lump in her throat, she matched her tones to his, 'To our voyage.' The wine was sweet without being too sickly; it had a tang that refreshed her mouth and Jay looked quizzically at her glass. 'This is nice, what is it?'

'My secret,' he laughed, 'but I guessed you'd like it. Drink up and have another.'

Jay shook her head. 'No, thanks, I'm not tempting fate. I've made a fool of myself once tonight and I don't intend repeating it.'

'We're all allowed one mistake,' he said softly, surprisingly, 'so long as we learn by it. On the whole I've enjoyed this evening very much. It's been a long time since I had such pleasant company.'

'Yes,' agreed Jay eagerly. 'Charlie and Jeff are fun. I like them.'

'I didn't actually mean those two,' drawled August. He leaned lazily back, his head turned towards her and his free hand resting along the back of the seat. Jay felt hot under his gaze but was unable to draw away her eyes. It was as though she was hypnotised. 'I meant you. Have I told you how delightful you look in that dress? If not I should have done. You're entirely different. I never realised that clothes did so much for a woman.'

'You're very kind,' murmured Jay, 'and I do appreciate you lending me the money.'

'Don't start that again,' he exclaimed impatiently. 'I don't want your thanks,' and then on a softer note, 'I really did mean you look stunning tonight—and'—he paused—'I'm glad you're being sensible about the drink.'

'Because of your wi——' Too late Jay clapped a hand to her mouth.

August stiffened and the familiar frown creased his brow. 'What's Charlie been saying? Trust a woman not to know when to keep her mouth shut!'

'Please don't blame her. She's your friend, really she is. She wouldn't have told me, only——'

'Only what?' he spat, his face dark now with anger. 'I see no reason why she had to mention Kate. That part of my life is over, forgotten.'

'Is it?' asked Jay quietly. 'Is it, August? Or is that what you try to tell yourself? As far as I can see your wife's still very much part of you. You've got this chip on your shoulder because of what she did and you're not man enough to cast it off. You regard every woman as another Kate without giving them the opportunity to prove otherwise. Let's face it, if I'd got really drunk tonight you wouldn't have found it amusing. It would just have confirmed your theory that I'm no different from the picture you've got of women in general.'

She expected him to come back with an angry retort, but instead his scowl faded and he pulled down the corner of his lips wryly. 'You could be right. I probably would have thought that. I'm glad I didn't.'

He took another sip from his glass and smiled. 'You're not really anything like Kate. The idea of travelling round the world on *Romany II* would have been completely abhorrent to her. The QE2 is more in her line.'

'If your tastes are so different why did you marry?'

'A good question,' said August reflectively. 'Let's say I didn't realise at the time. Kate changed as she grew older. When we were kids—I suppose Charlie told you about that?—she was one of us. We spent most of our time at sea, but her outlook altered. She became hard—the simple life suited her no longer. She was clever, though, and I didn't find this out until it was too late. I tried not to let it matter, but how can you go on loving a person who makes no secret of the fact that she only married you for your money—and either drinks herself insensible while I'm away, or entertains other men in my house to relieve her boredom, as she so indelicately put it.'

'Oh, August! I had no idea.' Jay's concern was clearly evident and involuntarily she touched his arm.

Whether it was relief that she knew the truth or whether he had planned it this way she did not know, but the next instant she found her glass being taken and August's arms pulling her close. Resting against his shoulder she felt the uneven thudding of his heart. Afraid to move for fear of spoiling this heavenly moment, she lay inert, content to allow her feelings for him to spill out, envelop her body and bathe her in a rosy glow.

When she felt his lips in her hair Jay thought her happiness was complete; it was not until he lifted her

76

chin and took her mouth in a kiss that was demanding yet gentle that she knew that what she had thought of as happiness was only the beginning of something much deeper. Why he acted in this manner when he himself had made the rule that theirs was to be a strictly impersonal friendship she refused to consider.

But her joy was shortlived when a few seconds later August pushed her roughly from him and going to the cabinet poured himself another drink which he downed in one swallow.

'That was a foolish thing to do,' he grated, more to himself than Jay. 'I don't know what came over me. I don't normally allow my feelings to get out of hand. I'm sorry—it won't happen again.'

'Don't apologise,' returned Jay softly. 'It proves you're human after all. I was beginning to have my doubts.'

He looked at her with swift suspicion, but his face relaxed when he saw her smile. 'Am I so difficult?'

'Sometimes—but perhaps now that you know I'm not like Kate things will be different?'

'You didn't mind me kissing you—after all I'd said?'

Jay shrugged and replied with a lightness she was far from feeling. 'What other way was there to round off the evening? I don't think any the worse of you for it. Now if you don't mind I'd like to go to bed. I'm very tired.' Which was a lie, for she had never felt less like going to sleep in her life. But how could she sit and face the man who had just regretted kissing her? It was clear he regarded her with no real affection—

his embrace had been reaction; his kisses meant nothing, and in all probability he would end up blaming her for leading him on.

He made no attempt to move as she brushed past him and her whispered, 'Goodnight,' met with nothing more than a brief nod. Behind the curtain Jay undressed in the glow from the saloon and slid silently into bed. August still had not moved. Her first instincts were to go to him; endeavour to make him understand that he couldn't go on dwelling on his unhappy marriage—*and confess her love*! This above all else she longed to do, and since his kiss, which had aroused desires that even Jay herself had not known existed, it was doubly hard to hide her feelings.

When he did move, instead of preparing for bed as she had expected August disappeared on deck where she heard him continuously pacing up and down as though he had some great problem that he could not resolve.

Surely not because of her? A kiss was a normal reaction for any man after a pleasant evening. The truth was more likely to be that he hated himself for letting his carefully assumed attitude slip. It proved he was not as strong a man as he thought.

At length Jay could stand his incessant pacing no longer. Heedless of the fact that all she wore was a thin nylon nightdress—one of her purchases earlier that day—she climbed out of bed and padded through the saloon. Lifting the hatch carefully, she paused while her eyes became accustomed to the gloom.

The glowing tip of August's cigarette revealed his

whereabouts a few yards away and without stopping to consider her actions Jay pulled herself up and tiptoed towards him. 'What are you doing? Why aren't you in bed?'

He swung round abruptly as if only then aware of her presence. It was too dark to see his face, but his voice was harsh, as when they first met. 'Is it any business of yours? What does it matter what I do?' It was almost as though they were strangers again, as if his attentions of a few minutes ago had meant nothing.

Jay flinched but maintained her stance. 'Contrary to what you may think I really am concerned. There has to be something troubling you, why else would you be here? Or'—with sudden insight—'is it me that's the problem? You can still back down, I shan't blame you.'

For a moment there was silence between them, the only sounds the lap of water against the sides of the ship, the odd creak as she moved on her moorings. Jay shivered, wishing she had stopped to wrap something round her shoulders.

'If only it were so simple'—began August, then peering at her more closely—'what the devil are you playing at? Get back quickly before you catch cold.' Without waiting to see whether she would obey he caught her arm and dragged her along the deck, almost pushing her down the steps in front of him.

Once in the saloon he thrust his discarded jacket at her and Jay accepted gratefully, only now realising how flimsy her garment was. Not that August had taken much interest, after one cursory glance he had entered the galley where he filled the kettle and was now spooning chocolate powder into mugs. 'Don't expect me to look after you if you're ill again,' he grumbled, 'I've never known a girl get up to so many tomfool tricks as you. Have you no sense?'

'How was I to know it had turned so cold?' Jay defended. 'Anyway, it was your fault for stamping up and down and keeping me awake—I was only trying to help. You know what they say about a trouble shared.'

'And I know what happens to girls who parade themselves in revealing nighties,' he returned. 'I don't know what you're playing at, but a man can only stand so much. If we're to be shipboard companions you'd better not wear that again. Choose something more practical.'

So much for her impression that he had not noticed what she was wearing! Jay did not know whether to feel flattered that he had entertained thoughts of finding her desirable—whether for the right reasons or not —or whether to be annoyed that he should try and dictate what she should wear. Ultimately she said nothing, causing him to glance at her sharply. 'I trust you're not sulking? It's for your own good I say these things.'

'Or yours.' His sarcasm caused Jay to automatically strike out in self-defence. 'We both know you're afraid of your own emotions, afraid to admit that the opposite sex still has the power to stir you. Let's get it straight once and for all. I'm not the type of person to encourage a man—especially one who I know has no feelings for me. I like feminine clothes and I dress purely to please myself. But'—in a smoothly condescending voice—'if it will make you any happier I will dress with the utmost propriety in future and wear nothing to cause you unrest.'

August swore beneath his breath and strode over to where Jay stood in the middle of the saloon. 'You little she-devil!' he grated, shaking her so violently that when he let her go the jacket fell to the ground. Her arms hung limply by her sides and for a second Jay was too astonished to say anything. The pink chiffon hid none of her firm young contours and when August deliberately and insolently looked her up and down she felt hot colour flame her cheeks. Swiftly, and before August could guess what was happening, she struck his face a blow that echoed throughout the tiny room. Then with a muffled sob she turned and reached for the curtain which would give her the privacy she so badly needed.

CHAPTER SIX

AUGUST'S hand closed on Jay's as she pulled the drapes to one side. 'You can't treat me like that and get away with it,' he rasped. 'You've asked for trouble and by golly you're going to get it! I ought to put you over my knee and spank you, but I think this will prove equally effective.' Mercilessly he threw her on to the bunk which practically filled the fo'c's'le, falling alongside her with a speed which left Jay no time to argue. His arms imprisoned her and his mouth roughly sought hers.

Jay tossed her head this way and that. 'August! What are you doing? Let me go!'

'Not until I'm satisfied that you'll play no more tricks like that,' he asserted. 'Isn't this what you want? Isn't it what you've been after all the time?' His breathing became heavy and uneven. Jay closed her eyes and tensed her body. There was no tenderness in his kisses now. Brutal and punishing, he savagely took her lips until she gasped for breath, and felt not a little afraid. Was this a foretaste of what the journey was to be like? Had she been wise to accept? Resolutely she kept her body stiff, resisting August with every ounce of strength. But despite his brutality, despite his complete disregard for her feelings, she could not help but respond. His very touch set her pulses racing until her head felt fit to burst. But she wouldn't give in. She daren't! He must never know how she felt. Not for anything would she give him the opportunity of saying, I told you so.

Her frustration ended in tears, and it was only then that August stopped. He stared at them slowly trickling down her cheeks, wetting her dark hair that lay awry on the pillow.

His lip curled. 'A typical feminine reaction, but as it happens I've finished. I trust you've learned your lesson. Goodnight!'

Shortly after that the boat was plunged into darkness and Jay turned her head into the pillow, trying to hide her sobs. August would never believe that her tears were sincere, that she had not turned them on as a means of allaying his assault. She knew she ought to leave the ship at once; forget all about this man who had ravaged her senses. But love forbade her make such a decision and she lay there in the darkness weeping silently, puzzling what madness had got into August and wondering what the outcome would be.

Sleep evaded her and judging by the movements on the other side of the curtain August too found difficulty in sleeping. She had never discovered exactly what was troubling him. Was it the thought of female company? If he had any doubts she had given him ample opportunity to change his mind. What else could be bothering him? His charter company, perhaps? It was all she could think of, but if he was not prepared to discuss it there was nothing she could do.

Eventually she slept; fitfully, restlessly. When she awoke it was to the sound of rain beating a steady tattoo on the deck and the smell of sizzling bacon coming from the galley. She pulled on her clothes—a wash would have to wait until August was out of the way—and stepped hesitantly into the saloon. She was not sure what to expect. August looked across, greeted her politely but indifferently, and carried on with his cooking. Determined not to reveal that the previous night's episode had upset her in any way, Jay said, 'Good morning, August, shall I take over?'

As if sensing her effort to smooth things between them he gave a brief smile. 'I've almost finished, thanks, but you can lay the table. How did you sleep? No after-effects from the drink?'

'None at all, though I seemed to lie awake for most of the night. You too. I heard you tossing and turning.'

'A guilty conscience,' he said drily. 'I owe you an apology.'

Jay looked across in surprise, but he concentrated on breaking eggs into the pan. 'Forget it,' she returned. 'Our acquaintance is too short for you to really know what I'm like. It was understandable that you should think I——'

'But it wasn't,' he interrupted tersely. 'I ought to have known better. It was just that I—oh, forget it,' and he banged the knife down viciously.

Jay deemed it wise to say no more even though she was bursting with curiosity. What could he mean? What had he been going to say?

Minutes later they were eating their breakfast in silence. August appeared uneasy and Jay racked her brains for something to say to ease the tension. She would rather have him in one of his moods than like this. At least she knew then where she stood. As it was she did not know what to think.

It was a relief when they heard scrambling sounds above and Charlie appeared through the hatch. 'Excuse me for barging in,' she called cheerfully, 'it's too wet to stand on ceremony.' In the few minutes it had taken to climb from one yacht to the other her hair was soaked and the plastic mac she had hung round her shoulders showered pools of water on to the floor. 'What a change in the weather! Have you a towel? I feel like a drowned rat.'

The difference in August was dramatic. He rose immediately to reach the requested towel, a broad smile creasing his face. 'Here, let me,' and without waiting for an answer he covered the girl's head and began briskly rubbing, and Jay, even though she knew Charlie was no rival, could not help but feel a stab of jealousy.

'Hang on,' laughed the blonde, 'don't tie it in knots!' She emerged flushed and laughing from beneath the coloured square and looked across at Jay. 'You'll have to teach this man of yours to be more gentle.'

Immediately August's smile faded. 'I apologise if I hurt,' he said abruptly. 'Maybe I'll leave you two girls to talk. As there's not much we can do today I'll have a chat with Jeff.'

Charlie pulled a face when he had gone. 'What's bugging him? Have you had a row?'

'Sort of,' admitted Jay, 'though I think you did it by calling him my man.'

'Can't see why.' Charlie reached for a clean cup and helped herself to tea. 'If you're going round the world with him I'd say you belong together even more than some married couples. There's no escape at sea.'

Jay nodded solemnly. 'I know. I've wondered more than once whether I'm doing the right thing. Sometimes I have no doubts, but other times I'm not so sure.'

'Such as?' queried Charlie, peering over her cup. 'You can tell me, I won't say anything.'

But Jay felt that by discussing last night's incident she would somehow be letting August down. She compromised by saying, 'He still thinks I had only one motive in coming aboard.'

'Heavens! I thought he'd got over that. What was it—the feminine touch?'

Jay nodded. 'That's why I'm back to trousers this morning. I shall stick to clothes like this in future.'

'It won't hide your charm,' smiled the other girl. 'Surely even August can see that?'

Flattered but unconvinced, Jay said, 'He wants a platonic relationship, full stop.'

'But how about you? Will you be satisfied with that —especially for so long a voyage?'

Jay assumed a blissful expression. 'To be with him is sufficient, except when he's rotten to me,'—this last said with determination—'but even then one smile and all is forgiven. Do you think I'm stupid?'

'You're in love,' smiled Charlie. 'We all do things

we wouldn't dream of doing otherwise. It's human nature, my dear girl.'

'Is it also human nature to fall for someone you hardly know—and what's more, someone who has hardly any respect for you?'

'Jay! You really are building up a sorry picture for yourself. I'm sure it's nothing like that. Give the man time to adjust. He's been a "bachelor" for so long he's forgotten how to treat women. In a few weeks you'll have him eating out of your hand.'

'Optimism again,' sighed Jay, 'but I hope you're right.'

The girls spent the rest of the morning chatting about the forthcoming voyage. Jay expressed doubts, but the blonde assured her that under August's instruction she would soon find herself a capable sailor. 'It's not as though you're completely ignorant,' she said.

Once again Jay kept quiet about her lack of knowledge.

The rain showed no signs of ceasing. It formed a grey curtain which almost obliterated land from view. Even the *Darling* appeared as a ghostly wraith at their side. Two hours passed before August returned, stiff yellow oilskins hampering his movements as he entered through the hatch, bringing a shower of rain with him.

When he had shed his wet garments he pulled a sheet of paper from his pocket and handed it silently to Jay. Her puzzlement changed to pleasure when she realised it was a reply to her cable.

Relieved to hear you are safe, it read. Money being transferred immediately. Father flying out with clothes.

Good luck on your voyage. It's a chance in a lifetime. Regards to August. Love, Mother.

Silently Jay handed it to Charlie and then looked across at the sea gypsy who was watching her with an amused twinkle in his eye. 'Not quite what you expected, eh? You thought they'd be over post haste to fetch you back?'

'Actually I did,' said Jay stiffly, wishing he hadn't weighed her up so accurately. 'I'm more than surprised they're taking it this way. But you never know, Father might change his mind by the time he gets here.'

'True,' admitted August with apparent unconcern. 'You'll have to fight it out between you.'

This was the escape she had sought. Jay's mind raced ahead to the possibility of returning to her home, her job, her friends—and she knew without a doubt that this was not what she wanted. Away from August she would be unhappy, frustrated. He was the only man she had ever loved and if it was within her power she had no intention of losing him.

'I'm coming with you,' she said simply. 'You asked me and I accepted. If anyone changes their mind it will be you.'

'Meaning you're afraid to opt out?' his face inscrutable, though Jay felt he was deliberately taunting her.

'Indeed no. You don't frighten me, August. I say exactly what I think.'

'So I've noticed.'

Charlie stood up then. 'Hey, you two, what is this? I thought you were friends.' She looked indignantly from Jay to August. 'You should be pleased that you have Jay's mother's blessing.'

'Oh, I am,' offered August solemnly. 'It's this little spitfire, she deliberately misinterprets everything I say.'

'I do not!' returned Jay hotly, before realising he was purposely baiting her. 'At least not always,' and she smiled wryly.

'That's better,' he grinned. 'You're so serious when I'm about. I don't eat little girls, you know.'

'You don't pamper them either,' interrupted his blonde friend. 'A woman likes a bit of fuss occasionally —in case you'd forgotten?'

For a brief second his eyes hardened and Jay knew that he thought of Kate. Then he relaxed. His lips curved and with unexpected swiftness he drew Jay into the curve of his arm. 'Poor child, I'm sorry. Let's say I'm out of practice.'

Charlie smiled, satisfied, and headed towards the companionway.

'Wait,' commanded August. 'Jeff's coming over— I've invited you both for dinner. It's such a miserable day we may as well make the most of it here. Think you can cope?' This latter question directed towards Jay.

She nodded confidently. 'Had you anything in mind, or will you leave it to me?'

August pretended to debate the question. 'I remember the last time you said that. Would it be wise, do you think?'

But Jay did not rise to his teasing on this occasion.

'That's a chance you'll have to take,' she responded gaily. All of a sudden the day had taken on a rosy hue. Even the rain held a charm, though had she been asked to explain why Jay would have found difficulty in putting it into words.

The next morning Jay's father arrived. Jay was sunning herself on deck—August having gone into Bénodet to do some shopping—when the taxi pulled up. She gave a squeal of delight when she saw James Gordon standing on the quayside looking hesitantly about him.

'Dad, here I am,' she called. 'There's our dinghy. Think you can row yourself over?'

Minutes later James Gordon stood in the saloon keenly observing his only daughter. 'I must say you look none the worse for wear—in fact I've never seen you look happier, but before I say anything else I want to see this man who's asked you to go careering round the world with him. I'm not sure that I like the idea.'

'But I thought—Mother said that——' Jay stopped, looked anxiously at the man who was so like herself. The same dark hair which only now in his fortieth year had begun to show a hint of grey; the same fine bone structure and green eyes, which at this moment in time were shadowed and unsure. He did not want his daughter to be unhappy, but it was evident that he had doubts about her circumnavigating the world with a man she scarcely knew. Jay herself realised it was an incredible situation but that arguing with her father would not help. He would need to be convinced that August was an honourable man and that his daughter would come to no harm while in his company. 'Speak to August yourself,' she said meekly. 'You'll like him, he's a nice man, Dad.'

'So I believe,' he answered drily. 'Both Rick and your mother seem to know him. It's only me who's in the dark.'

Jay frowned. It was the first time she had received any indication that her family knew the sea gypsy personally, but it made August's telegram less mystifying. But why hadn't he mentioned that he knew them? Still puzzled, she said brightly, 'There you are, then. If Mother approves it must be all right,'

'Your mother doesn't always know what's best,' James Gordon replied tersely. 'Things aren't the same as when we were young. No one's to be trusted these days.'

'August is,' defended Jay hastily. 'He's a fine man. He wouldn't harm a hair on my head.' She was thankful August could not hear her now; especially after the way he had behaved the other night. If her father ever found out! She went hot at the thought.

'Is this where you're living?' asked her father gruffly, glancing about the tiny saloon.

Jay nodded. 'It's a beautiful yacht, don't you agree?'

James Gordon snorted and pulled aside the curtain which hid Jay's sleeping quarters. 'It's not right you living here with that man. I never thought you'd do a thing like this.'

'But, Dad, you've nothing to worry about. Things have changed. Lots of people live together, and we're doing nothing wrong, if that's what you think. August sleeps here and I sleep there. We're friends, nothing more. August made that perfectly clear when he asked me to join him.'

Her father's eyebrows lifted. 'The man has more sense than I thought. Where is he?'

'He's gone into——' Jay paused and listened. 'That sounds like him now,' as a loud, angry voice hailed from the quay. 'I'll go and fetch him. Make yourself at home, I won't be long.'

'My father's arrived,' she said to August by way of explanation after taking one look at his scowling face. 'He's not very keen on me coming with you.'

'I guessed as much.' His face had cleared when he discovered the reason for the dinghy being missing. He flung his bags down before climbing into the boat himself. 'And you—what have you said to him?'

'I said you would look after me and he had no reason to worry.'

One eyebrow quirked. 'Thanks for the confidence. What brought that about?'

Jay shrugged. 'I want to come, it's as simple as that. As Mother said, it's a chance in a lifetime.' For nothing would she admit that it was August himself who was the attraction, that to be with this man was a desire stronger than anything else.

'I see.'

He sounded disappointed. Jay wondered if he'd secretly hoped that she would change her mind.

'In that case,' he continued, 'I'll see what I can do to convince him. Perhaps it would be best if you left us alone. Make some excuse to visit Charlie.'

Jay smiled and nodded. 'Whatever you say.'

They had reached *Romany II* when August suddenly said, 'I nearly forgot. I've bought you a present.' He pulled a bulky envelope from his pocket and Jay, flushed with pleasure, took it from him recalling Charlie's words that he never spoilt a woman and wondering if this had prompted his generosity.

What she had expected Jay did not know, but certainly not the book she now held in her hand. *Cooking Afloat*. Was it because she'd almost burnt the food yesterday? It had been his fault for distracting her attention, and consequently the meal had not been the success she had hoped. Trust August to rub it in! But she smiled politely, 'The very thing! How thoughtful of you,' and allowed him to help her from the dinghy.

Her father sat in the cabin looking very much the stern parent, and Jay's heart fell as she introduced him to August. The two men spoke quietly for a few minutes—friendly but distant, thought Jay. Time she left and allowed August to exercise his charm—of which she had as yet seen very little—on James Gordon.

The older man looked surprised when she announced her intention of calling on their neighbours. 'I did come to see *you*,' he said in a hurt voice. 'It cost a lot of money flying over here.'

Jay glanced at August, who gave an almost imperceptible nod. 'Don't worry, Dad,' she said, 'I won't be long. I must tell Charlie we won't be joining them for lunch after all.'

'Don't let me change your plans,' he put in quickly,

but clearly offended. 'I can easily go back to my hotel.'

'Oh, no, Mr Gordon.' August spoke decisively. 'I won't hear of it. It's a pleasure having you here. Jay's an excellent cook—she'll rustle up lunch in no time.'

'Really?' James looked surprised. 'I can't recall her ever doing any cooking at home.'

'Then you're in for a treat, Mr Gordon. Run along now Jay and tell Charlie we have a visitor.'

Jay spent as long as she dared with their friends, all the time wondering what was happening in the next ship. Was August winning? Had he succeeded in convincing her father that he was capable of caring for his daughter? It would not be an easy task, she knew, for her parent was a stubborn man.

It was with much trepidation that she eventually returned. But she need not have worried. August and her father were laughing loudly, tots of whisky on the table before them. They looked up as she entered, but August spoke first. 'Jim's been telling me about some of the tricks you got up to as a child. Seems this is not the first time you've been stranded at sea.'

Jay grimaced, recalling the occasion she had drifted out on an inflatable air bed and her parents had had to call out the coastguard. Not two weeks later the same thing had happened again, resulting in her being forbidden to take out the bed in future even under their close supervision. 'I suppose I am rather accident-prone,' she said.

August rolled his eyes upwards. 'Now she tells me! I can see I'll have to keep a close watch on you.'

James Gordon smiled fondly at Jay and pulled her

towards him. 'I'm not complaining. She's a good girl, but don't forget your promise, August.'

'Don't worry, Jim. She'll be safe. I don't take any risks when I'm at sea.'

The older man nodded. 'I realise that. I pride myself on being a pretty good judge of character. That's why I wanted to meet you, find out what sort of man had persuaded my daughter to make such a decision. I must confess I had my doubts.'

August grinned. 'Thought I'd held a gun in her back?'

'Something like that,' came the cheerful reply. 'Glad to see you're not like the usual boys she brings home.'

'Dad!' exploded Jay. 'What a thing to say! Anyone would think I brought a different one every week. Anyway, August's not my boy-friend, not in the way you mean. He's my——' She stopped, unsure what to call their relationship, and looked helplessly at the sea gypsy.

'Captain,' he supplied, the gleam in his eye belying his solemn expression.

'Aye, aye, sir,' Jay answered pertly. 'And what might your next order be?'

'I guess lunch. What say you, Jim? Are you going to sample your daughter's culinary efforts?'

'I most certainly am,' her father agreed. 'Though your mother will never believe me when I tell her.'

August moved towards the hatch, saying over his shoulder, 'I'll show your father the ship. You won't want us disturbing you.'

There was a meaning behind his words, but Jay did

not mind him taunting her now. The voyage was still on—that was all that mattered. Any day now they would be setting out on the next stage. She would be alone with the man she loved; completely alone, with only the sea and the wind as additional company.

Jay resolved there and then that nothing else would go wrong between them. But like all resolutions it was made to be broken, as she was soon to find out.

CHAPTER SEVEN

Two days later *Romany II*'s red sails were hoisted and she moved silently out of the harbour and along the River Odet. Once out in the open sea course was set across the Bay of Biscay for Vigo on the west coast of Spain.

August looked at Jay as she stood beside him in the cockpit. 'No regrets?'

'None at all. I once wondered what you got out of a life at sea, but not any more.' She looked up at the clear blue sky, felt the sea breeze brushing her cheeks, and knew that if necessary she could spend her life on board *Romany II*, so long as she had August for company.

Her companion smiled indulgently. 'We've hardly started. Wait until the bad weather when we get tossed about like a cork, and you can't sleep for the movement of the ship. See what you think then. That's when the true test begins. I expect all your sailing's been round the shores of southern England—am I right?'

Jay avoided his eyes and gave a slight nod, deciding that a swift change of subject was necessary. 'I was sorry to leave Charlie and Jeff behind. Do you think we'll see them again? Charlie said they were going as far as Tahiti.'

August nodded knowledgeably. 'Probably. One runs into all sorts of old friends at the various ports. And if you don't already know the people moored next door you soon do. They're a sociable lot.'

'I didn't realise,' said Jay. 'I imagined it to be a very lonely life, putting into port for supplies and then straight out again.'

'Is that a polite way of saying you thought I had no friends?' asked August. 'Is that how you see me—a lonely sailor whom no one likes?'

'Of course not,' flashed Jay. 'But—well, you said you preferred your own company and I naturally assumed that——' She shrugged and left the sentence unfinished.

'Now you see how wrong it is to presume anything until you have all the facts. Tell me, am I living up to my reputation?'

As usual his expression gave away none of his feelings and Jay was unsure what he was getting at. 'What do you mean? All I knew was that you preferred the sea to land—and that you liked to travel alone. I suppose you could say that the fact you asked me to join you proves you're not quite as anti-social as I'd imagined.'

He nodded slowly. 'I surprised even myself there—but it could turn out to be quite an experience. Kate's the only person who's ever crewed for me before. She didn't like it—and to put it mildly she left a lot to be desired. Maybe that's why I've never wanted anyone else.'

Jay found herself saying, 'Don't you think you're taking a risk—now? After all, you know nothing about me.' She was leaving herself wide open here, she knew, but it was too late to take back her words.

August smiled. 'It works both ways, so I reckon we'll both be on our guard and consequently get the best out of each other. But don't worry, you can relax for a while. I don't need your help yet. Get yourself accustomed to the boat and then when I do need you you'll be ready.'

The day stretched ahead. August set the automatic rudder and they sat together on the deck enjoying the sunshine while they could. A companionable silence settled over them and Jay lay back and closed her eyes.

Her father had stayed one more day in Bénodet, a day in which August had hired a car and showed them both something of Brittany's beautiful countryside. The two men got on well together, much to Jay's relief, and now that her father's objections had been overruled she felt able to relax and looked forward to the rest of the voyage with a clear conscience.

A few hours later she experienced again the stomach pains that had caused her so much discomfort in those first days on board *Romany II*. August took one look at her ashen face and ordered her to bed.

'It always happens,' he said, when he came down a few minutes later to ensure she had carried out his instructions. 'A few days in port and you lose your sea legs.' He filled a glass with water and handed her a tablet. 'Take this. I meant to give you one before we started.'

'What is it?' asked Jay curiously.

'An anti-sickness tablet. I got them in Bénodet. It will make you feel drowsy, but it will help.'

Jay was both surprised and pleased by his thoughtfulness, but felt too ill to dwell on it, and remembered very little for the rest of the day. In between periods of sleeping she nibbled dry biscuits, acutely aware of being yet again a nuisance to the sea gypsy.

'Don't worry,' he said, when she attempted to apologise. 'I'm prepared for it now. You're not the only one. It's a common ailment.'

It was dark when Jay woke again. Something had disturbed her. Before long she realised it was the movement of the ship. It rolled from side to side and she had to brace herself to avoid being flung against the sides of the forecastle. Weakly she called out to August, all the time doubting whether he would hear above the noise of the high wind and roaring sea and the peculiar bangings from up on deck.

But the next instant the curtains were dragged to one side. August grinned down at her. He was fully dressed and his hair clung damply to his head. 'The Bay of Biscay's never been kind to me yet. Think you can bear it?'

Jay nodded, tight-lipped, but her white, drawn face gave away the fact that the motion was doing little to help her sickness.

'Let me move you into the saloon,' he said kindly. 'There'll be less movement there.'

Glancing past him, Jay saw that he had already made a temporary bed on the floor with the foam pads from the settee. At any other time she would have suspected his motives, but now she was only too thankful for anything that would lessen her discomfort. He lifted her easily and helped her climb into one of the two sleeping bags. A rolled-up sail between the bags successfully wedged her and August between the seats, and surely enough the rocking motion of *Romany II* was less violent here.

Jay felt immediately better and although she had never before been at sea in such rough weather she had no fear. Her faith in August was unshakeable, and if he did not worry why should she? It did occur to her that he ought to be on deck in case they were blown off course or into the path of another vessel, but as he had crossed the Bay many times before, and obviously knew what he was doing, Jay felt completely safe.

In fact she was more afraid of her own emotions than anything else. Her nausea had temporarily disappeared, to be replaced by an increasing awareness of the man only inches away. She lay on her side, still and straight, every nerve end tingling with anticipation. She wondered whether he too thought about her, as a woman, and then dismissed the thought as unworthy. He had made it perfectly clear how their relationship stood and as his breathing gradually grew deeper and slower she knew that he slept. He obviously had nothing on his conscience to keep him awake, whereas Jay grew more aware of him with every second that passed.

Her own breathing became rapid and irregular and

she leaned up on one elbow with an irresistible urge to stroke his dark hair. In the gloomy cabin it was difficult to make out the outline of his face—not that it was necessary; every detail was imprinted in her memory for ever more.

She was not aware that he had opened his eyes and watched her curiously. When he spoke she gave a startled gasp and slid back into her bag, thankful for the darkness which successfully hid her heightened colour.

'Are you afraid?' he asked softly. 'Would you like to talk? It might help take your mind off the weather.'

'No, I'm not afraid.' At least not of the storm, she added silently. 'But I can't sleep.'

'I'm not surprised, considering you've slept most of the day. You're very brave. Kate used to dread storms.'

This was the second time he had openly compared her with his ex-wife, thought Jay. Was it a sign that his feelings towards her were changing? Was he beginning to realise that all women were not the same?

'I feel safe—with you,' admitted Jay. 'Though I'd be terrified on my own. Don't you ever feel that something might happen? You seem—so unconcerned.'

'I don't always get away scot free,' he said. 'I've had masts broken and sails torn to ribbons. I've been blown miles off course, but I've done all I can for now. This is nothing compared with some of the storms I've encountered.'

'Thanks for the warning,' said Jay with attempted lightness, while secretly dreading the thought of worse weather to come. Even now it felt as though the craft was about to break into pieces. It creaked and groaned,

102

sails slammed and tins in the store-cupboard rattled. She shivered. 'How much longer is this likely to go on?'

'It's impossible to say,' came the disconcerting reply, 'though you won't feel so bad in the morning. As with everything else it seems worse at night.'

He continued to talk reassuringly until Jay drifted once more into sleep. She did not know that he carefully brushed the hair from her face, or that he pulled the covers more closely about her shoulders.

It was light when she woke again. The cabin was empty. The ship still rolled, but the motion was soothing rather than frightening. Her illness had apparently disappeared and taking advantage of August's absence she washed and then dressed in one of the new green sweaters she had bought, complete with matching slacks. The colour echoed the green of her eyes and though she did not know it Jay looked more attractive than ever. Since their dispute over the nightdress she had been careful to wear only clothes that did not accentuate her curves, or add to her femininity in any way. Yet this morning, in the loose-fitting mohair jumper, she still contrived to look alluring.

She was brushing her hair when August lifted the hatch and lowered himself into the saloon. Quickly she pulled it back into a band, missing his frown and the swift tightening of his jaw.

'You're better, I see,' was his only comment as he rolled up the sleeping bags and stowed them away. 'Do you feel up to cooking breakfast?'

For the first time on their voyage Jay used the special belt to hold her steady in the galley, thus leav-

103

ing her hands free without the necessity to brace herself every time the ship rolled. Surprisingly cooking was not as difficult as she had anticipated. The stove itself was slung on gimbals with a guard rail to keep the pans in position. Before long she had turned out a very creditable mushroom omelette accompanied by grilled bacon and tomatoes.

Afterwards August suggested she join him in the cockpit. Pleased but apprehensive, Jay said, 'Is it safe?'

He laughed. 'Perfectly. I wouldn't suggest it otherwise.'

In fact it was a most exhilarating experience. Clad in oilskins, Jay wedged herself beside August and watched with excitement the mountainous waves as they washed over *Romany II*'s decks. The ship heeled over as she plunged at great speed through the seas. The water stung Jay's eyes and she tasted salt on her lips, but it was being in the middle of it all that stirred her most. They were truly at the sea's mercy, in the heart of nature in one of her most angry moods.

She glanced at her companion. He was clearly enjoying his fight with the elements. A smile hovered on his full lips as he carefully steered their course. His swarthy brown skin gleamed and his hair curled closely about his neck and ears. He had never looked so much like a gypsy as he did at that moment. All he needed, thought Jay, was gold rings in his ears to complete the picture.

For two hours they remained on top before she suggested a hot drink. At the same moment the wind increased in strength. 'We'll have to take in some more sail,' decided August promptly. 'You pull in another reef on the mainsail, while I take the staysail in altogether.'

Jay looked at him blankly. Her time of reckoning had come! August was already half out of the cockpit when he looked questioningly back. 'What's the matter? Are you ill again?'

Still she stared.

'Well, I'm waiting,' impatiently now.

'I—I don't know how.'

She thought he had not heard, until a wild oath was flung into the wind. His face darkened, eyes glittered. He lifted one arm. Jay braced herself and waited, but instead of the expected blow he pointed to the hatch. It was an order to go below. The questions would come later.

If Jay had ever felt like crawling into a hole and hiding it was now. The situation was entirely of her own making, she could blame no one, this she knew. If only there was some way out! If only it hadn't happened now, just as things were going smoothly between them. It was ironical.

The minutes crawled by as Jay waited. With each passing second her apprehension mounted. She sat on the edge of her seat, curled fingers digging into her palms; body tense, waiting. Would he turn her off at the next port? She thought it highly probable. Would he again think that she had worked her way on board—even though the final invitation had come from him?

A sudden lurch threw her off balance and she was on

her knees when August entered. His appearance mesmerised her and she froze, looking up with wide, startled eyes, like a fawn caught for one instant in the beam of a car headlight before suddenly darting away into the safety of the undergrowth. But she had nowhere to go. She was compelled to remain and face the angry sea gypsy.

'Get up,' he commanded, and then, 'Now, would you mind repeating what you said a few minutes ago?'

She looked at the muscle working in his jaw; at the black eyes, hard as coals, and the grim lips compressed into a straight, tight line—and trembled. She opened her mouth and tried to speak, but her words came out in a squeaky whisper. Swallowing, she cleared her throat and began again. 'I said—that—I didn't—know how.'

'How to what?' A staccato of sound in the panelled room.

'T-to—pull in a reef,' wishing the floor would open and swallow her up.

'Or hoist a sail? Or how to moor?' and as she shook her head at each question, 'In fact not even an elementary knowledge of sailing?'

Miserably Jay conceded this last query. 'I know I should have told you, but——'

'You *know*? I'm damn sure you should. To think I've landed myself with—with an incompetent, scheming, lying female!'

The loathing in his voice and the hatred mirrored in his eyes caused Jay to shudder, but it also had the effect of goading her into self-defence. 'I'm *not* a liar,' she said hotly. 'At least, I've only lied to you once, and that was all a lark—you already know about it.'

He folded his arms across his chest and studied her solemnly. 'In that case why didn't you admit you knew nothing about sailing? Wasn't it the obvious thing to do instead of letting me find out like this?'

'I wanted to,' cried Jay, 'believe me, I really did, but—well, I thought you wouldn't bring me then, and——'

He cut in harshly. 'You're so right, I wouldn't. Don't you realise that you're a hindrance now? A liability? There's no room for novices in the sort of voyage I have in mind. One has to be ready for any eventuality— and what's more important, able to react in exactly the right way. There would be no time for instruction if we faced a crisis. Your father's entrusted you to my care. What's he going to say if anything happens?'

'I don't know.' The fight was knocked out of her. He was right, of course. Wasn't he always? 'I hadn't thought of that, but—you do believe me?' Suddenly it became imperative that he should not think of her as a habitual liar, no matter what action he decided to take. 'You do believe that that is the one and only time I've ever told you an untruth?'

'As a matter of fact I do,' he said. 'Not that it makes any difference. The damage has been done.'

'And I didn't scheme or plot in any way to get on board,' she insisted. 'You can put me off at Vigo, I don't care, I'll find my own way home. But you must believe I'm not all those horrid things you called me.' Much to her disgust Jay's voice broke and tears filled her eyes. She dashed them away with the back of her hand. 'Please, August, please?'

'Spare me the melodrama!' he exclaimed impatiently. 'It doesn't help.' He passed a hand wearily over his brow. 'How the devil did I get into this mess? Why didn't I stick to my principles instead of letting a pretty woman turn my head? I might have known it wouldn't work out.'

Jay made a tentative gesture towards him. 'Don't blame yourself.'

But he brushed her hand away roughly. 'Don't touch me. In fact you'd best keep as far away as possible until we reach port, or I won't be responsible for my actions.'

This was the final humiliation. Jay turned and feeling her way blindly through the curtains flung herself down on to the bed. The tears ran freely now. There was no point in holding them back. No matter what she said August would only believe what he wanted. His faith in her had been shattered. She had tried so hard to make him see that all women were not the same. He had begun to mellow even, to treat her with more than the indifference he had at first shown—and now she had spoilt it all. Because of one silly mistake it was over. She could see no way out. Tomorrow, or the next day, they would reach Vigo. Her brief friendship, if she could call it that, would be at an end. Their few happy moments together a treasured memory. The lump in her throat threatened to choke her. 'August,' she implored silently, 'dear August, please be kind to me. I can't bear it when you're cross.'

At length she felt calmer and was able to view her

situation more clearly. It was evident that Vigo would be the end of her journey—but there was at least another twenty-four hours to be got through before then, and although August had told her to keep away Jay guessed that this had been said in the heat of the moment, for he knew as well as she that this was impossible within the narrow confines of *Romany II*.

Her only course, she told herself, was to eat humble pie, to apologise, state her intention of leaving the ship the moment they reached land, but that she hoped he wouldn't be too harsh on her for the remaining time they were forced to spend together.

With speech fully rehearsed Jay stepped out into the saloon. August sat on the bunk, head back, eyes closed, but as she approached he looked at her. She swallowed painfully. It was almost as though he cared—which was farcical under the circumstances. Must be wishful thinking, she told herself, that's what you want him to think. In reality he's glad you're going. His only disappointment is that once again he's been proved a bad judge of character. After this he will never, ever trust another woman.

'I want to apologise,' she began—but he let her say no more.

'The matter's closed. I'll fix your flight when we reach Spain.'

There was something in his attitude, in the way he spoke, that made her retort, 'If the journey's going to be so impossible why not make for the nearest port?'

'And go out of my way?' His voice held a note of

surprise. 'Vigo I've planned and Vigo it will be. Not even *you* will make me change that.'

God, he's stubborn, thought Jay. He doesn't want me, yet he won't upset his arrangements to get rid of me. It was like the journey to France all over again— only this time there was no hope of a reprieve.

'Suit yourself,' she shrugged. 'I was only trying to help.'

'You'll do that best by keeping quiet, but don't think you won't be asked to work. Even if you can't crew you can still cook and clean. I've been pretty lenient so far. I've given no orders, letting you do more or less as you wanted, but that will be changed. Until we reach Spain you'll do all the work that's not directly connected with the sailing of the ship.'

As if to add emphasis to his words *Romany II* heeled over more acutely than before, flinging both Jay and August across the saloon. Instinctively she clutched his arm. He helped her up, but moved away instantly as though her nearness revolted him. There was no time to reflect on this, however, as the interior of the ship was now in chaos. A door on one of the food lockers had swung open, throwing its contents across the galley and companionway. Tins rolled in a mixture of flour and brown sauce, and Jay looked at the mess in horror. She remembered now that she had closed the door but forgotten the latch which kept it secure at times such as this.

August too looked first at his normally tidy cabin and then at Jay's stricken face. 'Looks as though your job has begun,' he remarked with a mocking lift of those thick dark brows, before he shrugged into oilskins and disappeared through the hatch.

Jay looked after him, wishing she could develop a hatred to help her through these last hours. But it was no use; she could not force emotions she did not feel. She still loved August and consequently he had the power to hurt. She wondered whether he realised this; whether he was aware of her regard, or, a more likely answer, if he didn't consider her at all. He had probably mentally erased her from his mind, concentrating all his attention on getting them safely through the stormy seas. And if she didn't want to be in further trouble she had best start the cleaning up operation.

Jay's task was not helped by the movement of the ship. Each time she had almost got the tins back into the locker another lurch would send them scattering again. Tears of anger and frustration were not far away by the time she had finished. Her back ached with the continual bending and her head ached from the knock it had received when they fell. She had not been aware of it at the time, but now her fingers probed the area experimentally. It was swollen and felt tender to her touch. She took two aspirins and sat down, but as though he knew her plans to rest and was determined to thwart them August poked his head through the hatch. 'If you've finished I could do with a meal. See to it right away, will you, please?'

Jay dragged herself up, flinging an angry glance in his direction. She would have given anything to sit there for another few minutes, but obviously August intended working her fully, and not for anything would she complain. If he wanted to treat her like a slave, let him, she thought defiantly. No doubt he was trying to humiliate her; show her that no one could make a fool of him and get away with it.

Once again she felt close to tears and began to wish she had never heard of the sea gypsy. It was no fun loving a man who took no trouble to hide his dislike of her. To think she had once thought he might one day return her love! That was now all a faded dream. August would never allow himself such a luxury. He was afraid —he did not know it, but he was. Afraid to love again, afraid to let go of his tightly reined emotions. That was why he was so horrid most of the time. It was a barrier he had erected against the outside world—an impenetrable barrier so far as Jay was concerned. For she could see no way now of breaking through his defence.

CHAPTER EIGHT

FOR the first time since joining August on *Romany II* Jay wished for privacy, some place where she could shut herself away—and not by just a curtain. A locked door was what she needed, a place where she could give way to her emotions. She had never before felt so despondent. The rest of the voyage was going to be hell, she knew, for there was nothing she could do but feign a calm acceptance of the situation, an acceptance she was far from feeling.

August had eaten his meal in silence, Jay herself having no appetite and pretending an interest in a magazine she had found in one of the lockers. The words danced before her eyes, but she had religiously turned the pages. Judging by August's brooding expression and furrowed brow he would have had nothing pleasant to say in any case and she deemed it wise to keep out of his way.

As soon as she had cleared away the remnants of the meal she had declared her intention of going to bed. August had not even answered, and now she lay, still fully clothed, unable to give way to her anguished feelings. She had to be strong; she must not let August see that his annoyance still had the power to upset her. Not that he didn't have every right to be angry—he did—but need he carry it to such lengths? Was it necessary to treat her with so much contempt?

The sea had now ceased its turbulent wanderings and settled to a murmur and the boat sailed swiftly and smoothly through the waters. Jay listened as August moved about the ship and wished there was something she could say or do to lessen the tension between them. But he seemed determined to have nothing more to do with her and Jay sensed his impatience to reach Vigo.

Eventually she prepared for bed, but still she could not sleep. Neither, it seemed, could her companion. He moved about in the darkness like a caged animal and Jay longed to go to him. Couldn't he find room in his heart to be nice to her for these last few hours? He was obviously far from happy, so why prolong the agony? Why not call a temporary truce?

At last she could stand it no longer. Heedless of the fact that she wore only her pyjamas, Jay pulled the curtain to one side and stepped out into the saloon. The tip of August's cigarette glowed in the darkness and she addressed herself in its direction.

'For Pete's sake, August, we can't go on like this. I know I've done wrong and I accept the consequences, but can't we reach a compromise? This is ridiculous!'

His voice, bitterly sarcastic, came back out of the gloom. 'What are you suggesting? That I take you into my bed?'

Jay pictured the contempt on his face. 'Trust you to come up with an answer like that! The thought never entered my mind. I just want to be friends. Tempor-

114

arily, I know, but I can't stand much more of this and I'm sure you're not enjoying it either.'

The red glow moved nearer and she made out his shape as he stood a few feet away. 'How do you know what I like? I might prefer it this way. After all, I've managed with my own company in the past.'

'If your conscience is so easy then why aren't you asleep? I've never known you this restless before.' Jay wished he would put on the light. It was uncomfortable talking to someone she could not see. He drew on his cigarette and the increased glow momentarily illuminated his face. Although his eyes were still in shadow his anger was evident in the slightly flared nostrils and quick jerky actions. But Jay stood her ground. 'And don't say it has nothing to do with me, because you weren't like this before. Once your head was on the pillow you were away.'

'I'm flattered you noticed,' he said drily, 'and I wasn't going to deny that you are the cause of my discontent. Indirectly, of course. My main grievance is my own stupidity. I thought I'd learned my lesson.'

'And so you have,' answered Jay softly. 'I'm not here for what I can get out of you. Surely you realise that?'

'What else can I think? What have you done to make me believe otherwise?'

Subconsciously Jay took a step forward. 'You only have my word. Won't that do? Until we reach Vigo at least? You can think what you like after that—I won't be here to bear the brunt of your anger, but meantime, please, August, let's be friends. It's so—so humiliating when you treat me like this.' The darkness helped her now. It would not have been so easy to admit to her distress had they been face to face. 'I can't put up with it much longer.'

There was silence between them. August seemed to be weighing up the situation; trying to decide whether or not to succumb to Jay's plea. Suddenly he flicked his cigarette end to the floor and ground the butt out beneath his toe—a most uncommon thing for him to do as he was usually most fastidious in his habits. Jay waited apprehensively. It looked as though all her efforts were in vain, as if her attempt at a reconciliation had resulted in angering him further.

Tired of waiting, she turned back towards the curtain, her shoulders drooping dispiritedly. All that remained was to accept the situation as best she could.

'Very well!'

The words stabbed the darkness, causing her to stop abruptly. But she did not turn at once, she waited, expectantly; half joyful, half afraid.

'I'll try and forget. I'm not saying I can, mind. You've hurt me too deeply for that. But I see your point.' He paused significantly. 'Besides, it would be a pity to spoil this—your first trip in an ocean-going yacht.'

Jay clenched her teeth. Already he had taken the pleasure out of his agreement. Would he never be able to resist taunting her? 'Thank you,' she said tightly. 'Perhaps now we'll both get some sleep.'

This time her hand was on the curtain when he spoke again.

'Don't I get a goodnight kiss?'

Jay froze. What game was he playing?

'Surely if we're friends it's the obvious thing to do. I assure you it's done in all the best circles.'

'Perhaps.' Jay tried to ignore his sarcasm, and even more strongly tried to ignore the sudden erratic beating of her heart. The mere thought of August's lips against hers turned her legs to jelly, whether it was a kiss in friendship, anger, or pure mockery. 'But I don't feel like kissing you just now,' she lied. 'All I want is sleep.'

'Really? You surprise me. I thought you wanted much more than that. Why else have you tried to win my friendship?'

His derisive tones flicked her on the raw and she swung round savagely. 'You're despicable, Mr High and Mighty August! You think you're so clever. You think you know exactly what's in my mind. What a pity you're wrong. I wouldn't let you kiss me, not if you got down on your knees and begged. I hate you, do you hear, I hate you, and I shall be glad when I'm off this darned ship!' Tears ran freely down her cheeks. In her white-hot anger she lost all sense of direction and stumbled awkwardly against one of the lockers. 'Oh, damn! Why don't you put some light on in here?'

Her outstretched hand encountered August's chest. She shrank back as though she had touched red-hot coals, but before she could move away altogether his arms encircled her like a band of steel. It was impossible to free herself and struggling only succeeded in making his grip tighten. 'Let me go,' she gasped. 'You brute! What are you playing at?'

'I'm trying to stop you from hurting yourself.'

'Well, you won't do it like this.' Jay's voice rose hysterically as she attempted to escape. It suddenly became vital that she put space between herself and this man. 'Let me go!'

She was not ready for the swiftness of his actions. All she felt was the sting of his hand across her face. But it had the desired result. All her anger disappeared and she would have fallen had he not supported her. 'I'm sorry,' he said softly, 'but I had to do it. Forgive me.'

And as she lifted her face in wonder at the softness in his tones he kissed her, gently, as one would a child. Equally tenderly he brushed back her hair. 'You're quite a spitfire when you get going—and it's all my fault. I'm sorry.'

'You sound as though you mean that,' said Jay incredulously. 'I wish I could see your face. I wish I knew whether you were teasing or not.'

'This time I'm perfectly sincere. I assure you, Jay, I've never been more serious in my life.' He cupped her face between his hands. She could just make out his earnest expression before his lips closed on hers. Her response was immediate. Every fibre of her being burst into flame and unashamedly she clung to him.

Whether it was because of her reaction, or whether August himself had second thoughts, Jay did not know, for he released her with a swiftness that caused her to look at him in alarm. Never before had she met a man whose moods varied with such frequency. It was difficult to know where one stood with him. 'What's the matter now?' she asked hesitantly. 'Have you changed your mind?'

'No, no.' He fumbled in his pocket and she heard a match scrape before a flame gave a circle of light into the saloon. August held it to the oil lamp on the wall behind his head and soon the whole cabin was bathed in a golden glow. 'We can still be friends,' he continued, 'but I shouldn't have done that. I don't know what came over me, I ought to have known better. In fact I should have known *you* better.'

Jay frowned. 'And what is that supposed to mean?'

'Come off it,' he retorted thickly. 'Don't try and tell me you're not like that with every man?'

Jay opened her mouth to hotly deny this statement, but he silenced her with an imperative lift of his hand. 'If I'd given you any encouragement maybe I could understand, but as it is'—he shrugged expressively—'you ought to hate me. In fact, it was only a few seconds ago that you said you did. What's happened?'

'Sometimes I do, sometimes I don't,' admitted Jay. 'It depends on *your* mood.'

'I see.'

But she was sure he didn't. She wasn't even sure herself any longer. In that one second she had sincerely believed that she hated him. How could one love a man who took pleasure in making you feel small? Yet when he had kissed her her sentiments had changed as rapidly as the blink of an eyelid.

'And what are your feelings at this very moment?' His eyes flickered briefly over the pale green of her pyjamas back up to her face across which conflicting emotions were fighting for supremacy.

'I—I don't know,' she said at length. 'I feel confused.'

'You need a drink,' he said. 'Sit down and I'll make you one.'

Too surprised to refuse, or even to make any comment, Jay obeyed his instruction. He was in complete control of himself once again and showed none of the turmoil that had earlier ruled his actions. In fact he whistled softly to himself as he spooned coffee into two mugs. 'If you're cold,' he said solicitously, 'there's a sweater beside you.'

With the sudden realisation that she was shivering Jay accepted his offer with a smile. It was not only the woollen garment that gave her an instant warmth but the fact that it had once been worn by August. There was something intimate about sharing one of his jumpers and she hugged the thought happily to herself.

In what seemed to her only a matter of seconds the coffee was made and August sat down opposite her, his legs stretched out and his head resting idly against the wooden panel behind him. 'You're a strange girl,' he said, looking at her through half closed lids. 'I never quite know what you're going to do or say next. Life with you is certainly never dull.'

'I'm not sure how to take that.' Jay matched her tones to his, half serious, half bantering. 'I'd like to think it was a compliment, but coming from you I'm not so sure.'

'Meaning?'

'That you're not usually so free with your flattery. I've grown used to you condemning me and I've begun to expect it.'

August's lips twitched unexpectedly. 'You know your own faults, then?'

'I suppose I do, though generally speaking what might seem a fault to one person could very well prove an attraction to another. It would never do for us all to be alike.'

'Heavens, no!' he exclaimed. 'If I were like you I'd never survive.'

Jay grimaced. 'Thank you for those few kind words.' But she did not mind. The fact that August was speaking to her was comfort enough. No more of those long silences that had been hell to endure. She looked forward now with comparative calm to the remainder of the voyage. Vigo was the only place on which she would not let her mind dwell. The thought of their parting was like a knife in her back and she resolutely stopped herself from thinking about it.

They talked desultorily for an hour or more, yet although on the surface August had forgotten their disagreement Jay sensed a new reserve. This friendly attitude was all an act put on to keep her happy. It helped, there was no doubt about that, and hadn't she requested the truce herself? But there was an atmosphere; barely discernible yet there all the same, and when she eventually declared that she was going to bed she saw a flicker of relief cross his face. It was gone almost at once—he was keeping a very tight rein on his emotions, but she knew, and felt saddened, that he

121

could not relax sufficiently to enjoy her company.

It was not until much later when the ship was in darkness and August too had gone to bed that Jay recalled his statement that her revelation had upset him. She was suddenly wide awake. Surely this meant that he had begun to take an interest in her? Otherwise the fact that she could not crew would not have meant anything to him. Merely an anger that she had taken him for a ride, or so he thought, but his own personal feelings would surely not have been affected? Considerably warmed by this discovery, Jay snuggled down between the covers. There was hope after all.

The sea was still calm the next morning, with a strong following wind and they made good headway towards the coast of north-west Spain. True to his word, August was friendly—but no more. There was still that constraint which made it impossible for Jay to treat him with the frankness she desired. She had thought that during the remaining hours she might win back his regard—the warmth that had imperceptibly crept into their relationship. So many times she had to fight back a desire to reach out and touch him, to beg his forgiveness, implore him to take her with him as originally planned. Of course she couldn't. She knew that such a gesture would convince him once and for all that she had planned this trip right from the very beginning.

So the morning passed at a leisurely pace. Jay provided a cold lunch of meat and pickles, followed by chunks of fruit cake bought in Bénodet.

It was mid-afternoon when they saw land. August's smile widened as he pointed it out. Jay on the other hand felt as though the end of the world was near. Looking at her downcast face August said, 'Count your blessings, Jay. Life on board can be pretty miserable when the going gets rough and for a landlubber like yourself it would be unbearable, besides being dangerous.'

'I suppose you're right.' She lifted her shoulders disconsolately. 'I shall miss *Romany II*. I'd grown quite fond of her.' She would have liked to add, 'and of its owner,' but she knew that this was impossible.

August nodded. 'Me too, but then I've always loved boats, right from when I was a child.'

'Where did you live—in Devon?' It was the first time August had mentioned his childhood and Jay lost no opportunity in pursuing the question.

He shook his head. 'Folkestone. Though when my parents died I drifted from one place to another, eventually fulfilling my ambition to travel round the world. I did it the hard way the first time. I hitch-hiked, getting work where I could and food and lodging when I could afford it.'

'But you did strike it rich,' said Jay. 'Charlie tells me you own a charter company.'

'Trust Charlie!' he laughed.

'She only told me because she knew I'd—*thought* I'd be interested,' she finished lamely, hoping he hadn't noticed her slip. 'How *did* you get going?'

'It was luck, I suppose. I did a man a favour and he gave me an old cutter as a reward. She wasn't up to

123

much and it took me months and all my money to do her up, but I managed it—and that's how I started. Business boomed and now I can afford to travel round the world in the way I've always wanted.'

'Why do you do it?' Jay wished he was always so loquacious.

'Because I like it. The answer's as simple as that. Why does anyone do anything? If it's not to earn money it has to be for pleasure. If it's both you're very fortunate.'

The shadow of land had grown until the contours of the hills were clear. Greens and browns were now visible. But as they sailed along the coast towards Vigo Bay Jay was unable to appreciate any of its charm. Her only thought that this was the end of her association with August. It had been impossible to bridge the gap. August's reserve was impregnable. He was determined to carry out his plans and there was nothing she could do to persuade him otherwise.

They sailed into the calm waters of the beautiful Vigo Bay where they soon berthed and dispensed with the necessary formalities.

'It's a little late in the day to try and arrange your flight,' said August. 'I suggest we wait until tomorrow. Change into something suitable and we'll take a walk round the town and then find somewhere to eat.'

Jay was surprised by his offer and a little embarrassed, for she felt he was only doing it out of courtesy and not because he really wanted to. 'I don't want to put you to any inconvenience,' she said.

'I wouldn't ask if it did,' he replied shortly, 'but if

you don't fancy the idea it's all right with me.'

'Oh, but I do,' Jay responded hastily—too quickly, she felt upon seeing his raised eyebrows. 'I mean, it would be delightful, it's just that I don't want you to feel that you have to entertain me.'

'Don't worry your little head about that. I only do what I want—you should have learned that by now.'

Jay wondered whether she ought to feel cheered by his words. Instead he made her feel even more of a liability. Nevertheless she changed into a grey linen dress with its own matching jacket trimmed in red. She had bought it for just such an occasion but never dreamed that she would feel so unhappy wearing it.

August waited on deck. He had already changed into a dark lounge suit and Jay's heart fluttered unsteadily. Why was he so devilishly handsome? Why couldn't she have fallen in love with one of the boys back home? Life had been so simple then, so uninvolved. She had never imagined that love could bring so many problems.

Whether August approved of her outfit she did not know, for when she joined him his expression gave away none of his feelings. He smiled blandly and taking her elbow escorted her from the boat.

At any other time Jay would have been enchanted by the pretty town built in the form of an amphitheatre, but at present she was too full of her own unhappiness to appreciate its beauty. Even when August told her that according to legend the sea-bed here was covered by a layer of gold dating back to the War of the Spanish Succession she was unable to arouse any enthusiasm.

They climbed up to the Castro where they had a magnificent panoramic view of the city, later returning to the town where August led her to an attractive restaurant where he was apparently well known.

'You choose for me,' smiled Jay, after taking one look at the bewildering Spanish menu.

'Very well.' He inclined his head gravely and signalled to the waiter.

In Bénodet August had spoken fluent French, and she was not surprised now to hear his equally perfect Spanish. The mark of a much travelled man, she thought; perfectly at home in any surroundings.

For hors d'oeuvres August chose *jamón serrano* with ice-cooled melon, explaining that the ham was laid out in the sun on the snow of the mountains for the sun to cure it.

'It's perfectly delicious,' remarked Jay. 'Nothing like the ham we get at home.'

She said the same about the *Bacalao a la Vizcaina*, salt codfish cooked with fresh tomatoes, right through to the Almeria grapes she selected for her dessert.

Jay had been careful not to drink too much wine this time, but even so she felt heady with the excitement of romantic surroundings, Spanish guitarists playing flamenco music in the background, good food—and the right man. Her eyes sparkled and an unusual colour warmed her cheeks. Impulsively she leaned across the table, her hand resting lightly on August's arm. 'Thank you,' she said. 'Thank you for bringing me here. It's an evening I shall never forget.'

For a brief space he allowed his hand to cover hers

and there was a look in his eyes that Jay was unable to define. It was gone almost immediately and she was left with the feeling that he was deliberately shutting out his real emotions. He had relaxed for that one momentous second and a slight tremor had passed through his hand to hers.

'I'm glad,' he said softly. 'I don't want all your memories of me to be bad.'

'They would never be that,' she replied vehemently, slowly withdrawing her arm, 'rather the reverse. It's you who must think ill of me.'

'Disappointed,' he amended, his dark eyes studying her closely. 'Extremely so.' He sighed before continuing, 'If it will make you feel any better perhaps you might like to know that had I not been setting off on a long cruise I might have taken the time to teach you to sail. As it is——' his lips tightened, 'I have no alternative but to send you back to England. Would you like a brandy with your coffee?'

In other words, thought Jay, the subject was closed, but she did not feel quite so bad now. Those few words had heartened her. He could not hate her as she had feared; his reason for turning her off *Romany II* was purely for her own safety, nothing else. A bold thought struck her. Perhaps if she learned to sail during the time it took him to circumnavigate the world he would consider taking her on his next trip?

It was on the tip of her tongue to ask when she realised the stupidity of such a question. A lot could happen between now and then. August might even get married! An idea that brought a chill to her heart but nevertheless one which must be considered. She might even marry herself! Though the idea of meeting anyone who could remotely come up to August's standards amused her. Even so, there were those two possibilities which had to be taken into account. If only he would give her some encouragement. It wouldn't matter then how long she had to wait, so long as she knew that in the end August would be hers ...

CHAPTER NINE

AUTOMATICALLY Jay crammed clothes into her suitcase, her mind not on the job in hand but with the man on deck. It was midday. Her flight had been booked for early evening. Fortunately the airport was but a few miles away and while she finished packing August repaired one of the sails. She heard him whistling as he worked, and the very fact that he appeared cheerful by her impending departure caused her to feel irritable and almost like telling him to stop. All day he had been the same and although Jay had tried to match her mood to his it had been extremely difficult under the circumstances. As the minutes passed she felt herself becoming more and more agitated and finally, after snapping the locks on her case, she sat down and covered her ears with her hands, closing her eyes tightly and willing herself not to think any more about the sea gypsy.

'What's wrong?'

The words penetrated her silence and slowly Jay opened her eyes. August stood on the steps, a slight frown creasing his tanned brow. His hair stood at a rakish angle as though he had run his fingers constantly through it.

'Only your whistling,' she snapped, before she could stop herself. 'Do you have to be so cheerful? Couldn't you at least wait until I've gone?'

His brows rose. 'If you really object why don't you say? and just to keep the records straight I'm not whistling because you're leaving, merely because it's such a beautiful day. Doesn't the weather affect you? When it's grey and dismal I feel that way too, but when the sun shines it reflects right into my heart and I want to let everyone know what it's doing to me. I thought everyone felt better when the sun shone.'

'So you do have a heart? I'm glad to hear it, and no, I don't feel any better when the sun shines. At least not today, and you know very well why.'

August lowered himself into the saloon. 'Are you suggesting there's something I can do about it?'

Jay shook her head and feeling at a disadvantage with him towering above her pushed herself to her feet. 'I know there's not, but that doesn't stop me feeling low. I am human, you know, and I'm extremely disappointed that I can't come with you.'

'It's a pity you didn't stop to consider the facts before worming your way on board.'

'Don't say we're back to that again! You're impossible, August. I ought to be glad I'm going. I don't know why I let it bother me so much.'

'It's your pride,' he countered, 'nothing more. Once you're back in England you'll soon forget about me and wonder why you were so foolish.'

So that was what he thought. Jay's spirits dropped even lower. He had no idea how she felt, and although in one way she was glad, it hurt to think that he was taking her departure so nonchalantly.

'Perhaps you're right,' she said with an attempt at brightness, 'it would be silly to let a thing like this upset me. I mean, we've barely had time to get to know one another properly. You could say we were just acquaintances.' It tore her heart to say these words, but it was the only way. No woman with an ounce of pride would let a man know she loved him without some sort of prior encouragement; and this was sadly lacking as far as August was concerned. Even though he had put his present gay mood on to the weather Jay felt sure her imminent farewell had a lot to do with it.

She braced herself. 'I won't say I haven't enjoyed these last few days; I have, and I'm very grateful to you, August, for bringing me along with you. Especially for spending all that money on new clothes. I shall repay you as soon as I'm able, you can be sure of that.'

'Please,' he spread his hands eloquently, 'allow me to make it a gift. I too have enjoyed your company, despite the ups and downs. The cost means little, but your acceptance would mean a lot.'

He smiled, and Jay felt herself grow warm under his gaze. 'Thank you, if it will make you feel happier I'll gladly accept, though I'm sure I don't deserve your generosity.'

'Let me be the judge of that,' he returned a trifle gruffly. 'Do you think you could manage to conjure up one more meal before we leave for the airport? After today it will be back to my own cooking.'

The time passed quickly and all too soon they were

leaving *Romany II* and climbing into the taxi. Jay took one last lingering look as she lay gently bobbing on her moorings, at the sparkling white deck and the red sails neatly furled, and knew that she would never forget this beautiful ship, or the man who owned her. They held a special place in her heart and would be there for as long as she lived.

Through the rugged countryside they rode though Jay saw nothing of its beauty. Her eyes stared blindly out of the window, her hands clenched tightly in her lap and she tried hard to swallow the lump that persisted in rising in her throat.

She was very aware of August sitting at her side, of his thigh almost touching hers and the fact that he too was tense. She wondered why. Her own reason was simple to analyse, but August—he had been so blithe a short while earlier—what was the matter now?

A tangible silence settled between them. Jay feared to speak in case she gave away her true feelings and August—he just sat there, staring straight ahead almost as though she did not exist. The girl stole one or two glances in his direction, noted the hard lines on his face, and his expressionless eyes staring into the distance. He did not appear to notice her curiosity, so engrossed was he in his own thoughts.

They had almost reached the airport before he said, 'Do you mind if I don't wait to see you off? I hate goodbyes and I'd rather get it over quickly.'

Jay did mind. She minded a lot, but was too polite to say so. 'No, of course not. I'll buy a magazine and settle myself in a corner until my flight's called. You've

132

no need to wait at all. When do you intend leaving Vigo?'

'Straight away,' he said promptly. 'I have all my supplies, so there's nothing to keep me now.'

Jay forced a smile. 'I wish you good luck. I hope everything runs smoothly.'

'I have no fears. *Romany II*'s never let me down.'

They were at the airport by this time. August asked the taxi driver to wait while he carried Jay's case into the departure lounge. He waited until she had checked her baggage through Customs; made sure she had sufficient money, then took both her hands firmly in his.

'Goodbye, Jay. I'm sorry it's turned out like this, more sorry than you'll ever know. Look after yourself.' He looked deep into her eyes before turning and walking swiftly away.

The tears that had threatened for so long welled over and as Jay looked after him all she saw was a misty blur. He had walked out of her life! He had not even kissed her goodbye, nor did he look back to give a last minute wave. It was more than she could bear. Sobs broke in her throat as she made for the cloakroom. Mercifully it was empty and she allowed her grief to wash over her. This parting was worse than she had imagined. How could she ever put on a brave face again? What else was there left to live for?

In the end she had to force herself to calm down. She splashed her face with cold water and renewed her make-up. Life had to go on.

It was as she ran the comb through her hair that she

heard the announcement. Her flight had been delayed for two hours!

'Oh, no!' she cried aloud. '*Oh, no!*' It was bad enough leaving without an enforced wait to add to her misery. Slowly, feet dragging, she walked from the room. She bought a magazine and finding a quiet spot sat down in readiness for her long wait.

It was difficult to concentrate and after a while the book lay idle on her lap. She watched the doors, saw people coming and going; some happy, some sad like herself, but all the time it was August's face she saw—superimposed on every person. Yet never once did he look her way. He was no longer interested. She was a ship that had passed in the night. He had his own life to lead and Jay formed no part of it.

At this juncture in her thoughts she heard her name called and almost at once a breathless Charlie threw herself down beside her. 'Thank goodness I caught you in time!' the blonde panted. 'August said I was a fool to try and that you'd be well on your way to England by now.'

'And so I would if the flight hadn't been delayed. But why have you come? I take it August's told you the whole story?'

'Too true he has.' Charlie sounded angry. 'I wish I'd been there at the time. I'd have made him see sense.'

Jay smiled wryly. 'You can't blame August. He's within his rights—and besides, I should have to be a liability.'

'As if you ever would!' Charlie's fine brows arched disbelievingly. 'August can sail that yacht single-handed, as well you know. He doesn't need a crew. It's company more than anything else that he wants. I'm convinced that's why he asked you.' She shook her head determinedly. 'I've been fuming all the way here. If I hadn't been in such a hurry to catch you I'd have told him exactly what I thought.'

Jay sniffed. 'I doubt it would have made any difference. He was determined to get rid of me. Perhaps he realised he'd made a mistake and used the fact that I knew nothing about sailing as an excuse.' She sighed deeply. 'It's nice to see you again, Charlie, but there's nothing you can do. It's all over between August and me. If you were thinking of taking me back to Vigo to try and patch things up you can forget it.' It was a tantalising thought, but there would be no point in attempting a reconciliation—of that she was perfectly sure. August had had ample opportunity to change his mind.

'No, it's not that. In any case it's too late. He was preparing to leave as we berthed.'

'Then why are you here?'

Charlie studied her nails with assumed indifference. 'It seems such a pity for you to return to England. What you might call an anti-climax after your expectations of a round the world trip. Jeff and I thought that—well, at least I thought, and I'm sure Jeff will when I tell him —that you might like to come with us? It won't be anything like what August offered. Tahiti's as far as

135

we're going, but I know you'll enjoy it. What do you say?'

Jay hesitated; liking the idea but uncertain about the advisability of accepting. There was a strong chance that they might encounter the sea gypsy again and undoubtedly he would think that she was still following him. She did not want to help fertilise the seeds already sown in his mind. 'Thanks for the offer, but I couldn't.'

'You think you might bump into August?' questioned Charlie intuitively. 'I doubt it. In the mood he's in he'll press on without a stop for as long as his provisions last. Please say you'll come. Who knows, you might learn enough about sailing to be able to go with August on his next trip.'

'I wouldn't dare ask him,' laughed Jay, loth to admit that her own thoughts had run along similar lines. 'How long do you reckon he'll be away?'

Charlie shrugged. 'A couple of years. Maybe more, maybe less—it's difficult to judge. A lot depends on how much time he spends ashore, but you still haven't answered my question.'

'I'll come,' offered Jay. She had known all along that her answer would be yes, and that deep down there was only one reason, but she wouldn't admit this—not to anyone, not even herself.

'Good.' Charlie sprang up. 'Get your bags and let's go.'

Jay clapped a hand to her mouth in sudden horror. 'I can't. My case has already gone through. They won't let me have it back now.'

'Then let it go,' replied Charlie cheerfully. 'I've

enough clothes for the two of us—most of them new—
so you can take your pick.'

Jay felt bemused by the way things were being
taken out of her hands. 'You're very kind. How can I
pay you back?'

'You don't have to. I'm doing this because I like
you and——'

'You feel sorry for me?'

'I didn't say that, but if you don't hurry I'll make
you pay for the taxi, he's still waiting.'

Jay looked horrified. 'Heavens! It will cost a fortune. You must let me go halves.'

'You'll do no such thing. It's not your fault. Come
on, let's go.'

Minutes later they were speeding back along the
route Jay had covered earlier. Once again she saw
nothing of her surroundings. She felt completely bewildered by the sudden turn of events. Going back with
Charlie was infinitely preferable to returning home. It
would have been embarrassing to say the least to have
to admit to a dispute with August so soon after their
meeting; but all the same there was not the same excitement as she had felt when anticipating the voyage with
the sea gypsy. It had been the man, not the journey,
that had stirred her senses. Jay admitted this now.
Never had any other man aroused her in this way, and
the thought that he had gone out of her life filled her
with a despair that was difficult to dispel. Even
Charlie's generosity failed to cheer her and although
she did her best not to let her friend see how sad she
felt it was difficult not to give way and allow the tears

to once again tell their own story.

They soon reached Vigo, and as they neared the harbour Jay felt her heartbeats quicken. August might still be there! A slim chance, she knew, but one that could not be ignored.

Her whole body tensed as they rounded the last corner and it was not until she saw the empty berth that she let out a sigh of relief—or was it disappointment? Only her heart knew the truth, and this she firmly denied herself.

A chuckle of amusement from her friend told Jay that she was being observed.

'Did you really expect August to be here?'

'I hoped not—but something could have delayed him.'

'You wished it had?'

'Gosh, no,' cried Jay. 'It would be too humiliating.'

Charlie's lips quirked. 'Poor Jay! Never mind, I'm sure you'll enjoy yourself with us. Here's Jeff now, wondering what's going on. I didn't stop to tell him.'

'Where have you been?' he called as Charlie stepped out of the taxi, and then as Jay appeared close behind, 'What's going on? I thought you'd gone with August.'

Jay looked swiftly at the blonde, who, after paying the taxi driver tucked her arm lovingly through Jeff's. 'I'm sorry, darling, I hadn't time to explain. I thought August might tell you.'

Jeff ran his fingers wildly through his hair. 'August left as though his life depended on it. I thought it strange Jay wasn't in sight. What *is* going on? Won't someone tell me?'

'Poor darling. Let's go on board and I'll explain everything.'

They spent a further three days in Vigo, during which time Jay's hopes of seeing August again slowly dwindled. Every passing hour increased further the distance between them. With due respect for her friends Jay made a tremendous effort to appear carefree and happy, but although Jeff seemed convinced his wife certainly was not.

'I wish you wouldn't let that man bother you,' she said to Jay one night as they were taking a stroll before supper. 'There's nothing you can do and you'll only make yourself ill.'

'I wish I *could* stop. I keep telling myself I'm a fool; that August's gone out of my life and I mustn't think about him. But it's not so easy. I can't help myself. I love him dearly and I'd give anything to see him again.' She sighed deeply. 'Why couldn't I have fallen for some nice guy who loved me in return?'

'Life would be awfully dull if we could plan things the way we wanted them,' counselled Charlie. 'It's part of the game to fight for what we want.'

Jay's brows rose comically. 'How can I fight without an opponent?'

'Your turn will come. You've had one bout—and lost —but there'll be a return match, I know, and next time you must be sure to win.'

'*If* there's a next time,' scoffed Jay. '*I'm* certain there won't—not if August has anything to do with it. If he ever finds himself anywhere near me he'll head in the opposite direction without delay.'

Charlie snorted. 'You're a defeatist. Here am I trying to cheer you up and all you do is throw it back in my face!'

'Sorry,' grinned Jay ruefully. 'I didn't mean to. If only I could learn to hate him. Tell me something bad about August.'

'There is nothing,' replied her friend. 'He's a good man in every way. I've never understood why you two don't get on. You're ideally suited.'

'We're too much alike, that's the trouble. Neither of us would ever concede that we were not right.'

Charlie looked pensive. 'There has to be give and take in every partnership—otherwise that's where things go wrong, especially with people like you.'

Jay acknowledged the truth in her friend's words, yet even so, had she tried her best not to argue, she did not think it would have altered things. August was determined not to like her. All she was certain of now was that she must try even harder to push him from her mind.

During the remaining days in port Jeff taught Jay much about sailing. Whether he too thought it might help if they ever met August again, she did not know, though she was grateful for his tuition.

'I realise it all sounds very complicated,' he said, after explaining how to pull in a reef, 'but once we get under way I'll let you put your theory into practice—that is if you want to—you don't *have* to help out.'

'I'd love to. It might come in useful—one day.'

He looked at her thoughtfully but said nothing. Jay

guessed he was thinking about August.

'I don't want to make a fool of myself again,' she finished lamely.

'It beats me why you ever let August believe you could crew. It was a foolish thing to do.'

'I realise that now. I didn't know he was so hot-tempered.'

'He's not normally. I've rarely seen him upset.'

'Then it must be me, for we hardly spent a few hours together without arguing.'

He looked at her in surprise. 'I thought you were happy together. Why else did he invite you to crew for him?'

'I've no idea. I hoped it was because he liked me—now I know he doesn't. I was a fool ever to think he might——' Jay broke off, suddenly realising she had given away too much.

'Love you?' The bearded man looked compassionate. 'Charlie told me how you feel and if it's any consolation I agree with my wife. August's a fool, but he'll come to his senses, you wait and see.'

'How easy you make it sound. Don't you realise he's hundreds of miles away? I'll never see him again—unless it's when he returns to Brixham, and by then he'll have forgotten all about me.'

Jeff's bushy red brows rose. 'After the impact you made? I doubt it.'

That night Jay wished she had not accepted Charlie's invitation. Their whole way of life was a constant re-minder of August and it was inevitable that his name should be frequently in the conversation. She lay awake for a long time trying to decide whether to return to England before it was too late.

Usually the gentle movement of the ketch lulled Jay into sleep, but on this occasion it evaded her. In the end she climbed out of bed and shrugged into a warm coat. Tiptoeing carefully through the saloon where her companions were sleeping, she climbed up on to the deck and here let the cold night air wash over her.

Turning her face towards the open sea, she looked out into the inky blackness. Somewhere out there was the *Romany II*—and August! Her heart sent a silent appeal for him to return; to forgive her indiscretion and let her join him once more on his voyage. How long she stood there she did not know; it was not until she was shaking with cold that she returned to her bunk. This time sleep came and with it a blessed relief from her torments.

The sun across her face woke her. It seemed only minutes since she had gone to sleep and it took a tremendous effort to drag herself back into wakefulness. She could hear Charlie and Jeff moving about and knew that it was time she was up.

Somehow her problem did not seem so great this morning. As with all troubles it had assumed greater proportions during the hours of darkness and now she was able to laugh at herself for even considering returning to England.

Someone had turned on the radio and the sound of a current pop song caused Jay to hum the tune softly to herself as she dressed. She vowed there and then to push the sea gypsy from her mind and enjoy herself.

The song was true. Broken hearts did mend—if you wanted them to. But not if you went on grieving.

She stepped into the saloon and greeted her friends with such a carefree air of abandon that they both looked at her in surprise.

Jeff was the first to recover. 'There's no need to ask how you're feeling this morning. Would it be rude to ask what's brought about the sudden change?'

Jay shrugged and assumed an innocent air. 'What do you mean? I'm no different.'

'Come off it,' interposed Charlie. 'You look as though you've lost a penny and found a pound. What's happened? You have a good dream or something?'

Jay smiled. 'I've turned over a new leaf, that's all. My life is beginning from right now. The past is forgotten.'

'Good girl!' Jeff was enthusiastic. 'I'm glad you've come to your senses. We're leaving right after breakfast, so you can help Charlie stow away the gear while I sort things out on deck.'

Jay was glad of the extra work and when they eventually sailed out of Vigo harbour she felt no regrets. Today was the first day of her new life and she was determined to enjoy it.

Under Jeff's instruction she hoisted sails and generally made herself useful about the boat. She experienced again the exhilaration of wind against canvas; of the vessel cutting cleanly and smoothly through the water leaving a white vee in its wake. She stood on the bow and lifted her face to the breeze, revelling in the occasional spray that showered over her.

To those who watched it was as though she really had forgotten her former love. She looked as if she had not a care in the world. Only the girl knew that it took all her will power to create this impression. She forced herself to keep busy, not allowing a minute when she might dwell on the sea gypsy. She knew that the nights would be the worst times, when the blackness took over and she was left with nothing else but her thoughts.

For the moment, however, she was happy, despite a recurrence of her seasickness, and revelled in this healthy outdoor activity. They spent many days at sea, quiet, uneventful days when it appeared nothing could go wrong. Jeff had initially planned to stop off at Casablanca, but as they had made such good headway and the weather was in their favour for the Atlantic crossing they unanimously decided to head straight for Las Palmas.

The following day they wished they had stayed on their former course. Black, menacing clouds replaced sunny blue skies and the wind increased steadily. Jay had her first practical experience of pulling down a reef in the mainsail.

They all three stayed on deck, dressed in oilskins to protect them from the heavy spray which now constantly washed over the vessel. Jay was excited. Now that she knew more about sailing and felt that in some small way she could help she was not afraid. The increasing swell on the sea only served to bring an alertness to her senses and she was ready to carry out any order Jeff gave.

144

As the day progressed so too the wind increased in strength. Low black clouds raced close to the surface and they were forced to pull in another reef in the mainsail and take in the jib completely. By now fear had begun to replace Jay's stimulation and when Jeff suggested they go down below she made no demur.

Despite the movement of the ship they managed to cook and eat a meal, and as the *Darling* was set on automatic pilot and there was nothing they could do except let it ride out its course they settled down to try and sleep. As on the occasion when Jay had been in a storm with August, they put mattresses on the floor in the saloon where there was the minimum of movement and all three huddled together.

Surprisingly Jay went to sleep almost immediately, but when she awoke several hours later it was to find the wind really screaming. Jeff was missing, but he returned a few seconds later, having been on deck to take in the rest of the sails.

The violent motion of the ship now caused Jay to look at her companions in horror. She wanted to ask what their chance of survival was, then thought it best not to know. If she was going to die at sea she would rather not know. Jeff himself did not seem in the least perturbed, and Charlie, although her face was whiter than usual, had an air of calmness that somehow instilled a little confidence into Jay. Perhaps all was not lost.

And then suddenly, without any warning, they felt a terrifying crash; daylight changed to semi-darkness and a stream of water came through the hatch which had been wedged open for an inch or two so that they could get some fresh air.

Jay heard herself scream. It was like a nightmare—a horrifying dream from which there was no escape. The water poured in as though it would never stop. 'What's happened?' she rasped. 'Have we hit something?'

'We're buried under a wave.' Jeff's voice was hardly audible above the noise of the storm. 'It will stop—in a minute.'

But to Jay it seemed as though this would never be. The water continued to rain down on them until it was ankle-deep. Fear parched her throat and her eyes were riveted to the narrow space through which an incredible amount of water forced its way.

After what seemed an eternity it did stop. Full daylight returned to the cabin. The water washed back and forth with the movement of the ship and Jay wondered how they would set about cleaning up the mess. Through the porthole she could see the mountainous seas looking as if any minute they would pour over them again. Jeff lifted the hatch and pushed his head through. The wind tore at his hair and he had difficulty in breathing, but he soon got to work on the bilge pump and Jay was glad to see that the water quickly disappeared. Neither of the girls had spoken during this alarming experience and now Jay clung weakly to the nearest support saying, 'I never thought we'd come out of that alive. Does this happen regularly?'

Charlie shook her head, her blonde hair clinging in wet strands to her face. 'I've never been in a storm like this, though I've heard stories of ships who have been lost in such gales or who have limped to the nearest port with so much damage that it's been a wonder they have ever made it.'

Jay's eyes were wide. 'Do you think we've suffered?'

'Keep your fingers crossed. Jeff will soon tell us.'

But Jeff's news was good, as far as he could tell. He said it would be impossible to make a proper inspection until the storm had blown itself out.

For several more hours they were buffeted and tossed by the violent seas, none of them feeling much like talking, and the strain beginning to tell on their faces. Gradually, however, the wind moderated and Jeff suggested they try and get some sleep. 'There's nothing we can do before morning,' he said. 'Let's hope for better weather then.'

His prayers were answered. They woke to beautiful sunshine and blue skies. The seas were still high, but it was almost possible to see them gradually flattening and by mid-morning they could not have asked for better sailing weather.

They put out clothes and bedding to dry in the rigging. Jeff cleaned out the bilges and soon it was impossible to tell that there had ever been any mess. Only the mattresses had to be discarded. 'Sea water ruins them,' said Jeff as he flung them over the side. 'You can never get them back into shape.'

Once order had been restored and there was little for them to do except enjoy the remainder of their voyage to the Canary Islands Jay realised with faint surprise that for the past thirty-six hours she had not once thought of August. She wondered now whether he had experienced any such difficult crossings and felt quick sympathy for him travelling alone. She herself had known fear, even with company, but by herself she would have been absolutely petrified. It was an ordeal she would not easily forget.

It was mid-afternoon when Jeff pointed out the distinctive three peaks of the mountains around Las Palmas as they appeared above the horizon. Two hours later they sailed into port and anchored in front of the yacht club. Not surprisingly Jay had scanned the area for any sign of *Romany II*, breathing more easily when she failed to find her.

They stayed only one night in this capital of Grand Canary—with its splendid Las Canteras beach, exotic nightspots and fascinating shops. The next morning Jeff suggested they move to a quieter island where they could spend a few lazy days soaking up the sun and swimming—or doing whatever else they fancied.

The two girls were enthusiastic, both agreeing that this city was not their idea of a relaxing holiday, and before long they were gliding back out of the inner harbour. It was clear that Jeff had covered these waters before, and content to let him find his own way, Jay and Charlie lay down on deck enjoying the warmth of the sub-tropical sun. Jay was glad now that she had not returned to the cold damp of an English winter and closed her eyes, luxuriating in her new-found freedom.

A smothered exclamation from Jeff brought the girls to their feet, and what Jay saw caused the colour to drain from her cheeks.

CHAPTER TEN

'PLEASE turn back,' Jay implored. 'Please! We can't stop here.' Not when the one man she wanted to avoid was moored right alongside.

'I can't go now,' Jeff said apologetically. 'We've probably been seen.'

'Then I'm going below.' Jay prepared to move. 'And I shall stay there until either he goes or we do.'

'Jay,' protested Charlie, 'don't be so unreasonable. He won't hurt you.'

'His tongue will,' flashed Jay. 'You've no idea.'

'Then I'll tell him it was my plan,' insisted the blonde, 'and that you had nothing to do with it. He'll believe me.'

'Perhaps.' Jay sounded unconvinced. 'Anyway, I'm moving from here. The longer I can put off the evil moment the better.'

Through the porthole *Romany II* was clearly visible, and at this hour it looked deserted. If only Jeff would take pity on her and sail away to one of the other islands. August need never know they had been here.

First appearances turned out to be true. The yacht *was* unoccupied. Charlie hailed and then explored, only to return shaking her head. 'Must be on the island somewhere. Let's go and have a look around ourselves. This is a wonderful place, too good to miss.'

But Jay hesitated. 'What if—what if we see August? What shall we do then?'

'Be perfectly natural, of course. It's quite common to meet one's friends several times on a voyage such as this. I'm sure he won't accuse you of any ulterior motives.'

Deciding it was not worth arguing, Jay reluctantly climbed up on deck, warily looking about her and now altogether convinced that August was not lurking somewhere in the shadows.

It was indeed a beautiful island; rugged and wild with lofty volcanic mountains and vigorously cultivated fields, but as with Vigo Jay was too unhappy to appreciate its splendour.

They spent an hour or two exploring before returning to the *Darling*. They were met by one of the islanders, an old man with a lined brown face and a toothless smile. He burst into rapid Spanish, but when he was met by blank stares asked in halting English whether they knew the man who owned *Romany II*.

'Yes, we do,' responded Jeff. 'He's a friend of ours. Is anything wrong?'

'He is ill—very ill.' The man appeared agitated.

Jay's hand rose involuntarily to her throat. August ill! She must go to him. All thoughts of their conflict fled. If there was anything she could do——

They began to follow the man as he turned back in the direction of the village, but he stopped and pointed to the two girls. 'Not you. Only him.'

Jay looked beseechingly at Jeff, but he shook his head. 'Best wait. I'll see what's the matter and let you know. Perhaps later——'

The girls stood and watched their retreating backs and then Jay turned to her friend. 'What do you think? He said he's very ill. What if he should——'

'Don't talk rubbish,' cut in Charlie. 'He's most likely picked up an infection or something. The man's probably exaggerating.'

'I wish we could see him. Why wouldn't he let us?'

'Don't ask me,' returned the blonde, 'but it won't do any good standing here worrying. Let's make a drink.'

The next hour was the longest Jay had ever spent. All kinds of horrifying thoughts passed through her mind; the most disturbing of which was that in some indefinable way she was responsible for August's mysterious illness.

'What do you think's keeping Jeff?' she asked repeatedly. 'What's he doing? Why doesn't he come?'

'Look,' said Charlie patiently, 'all we can do is sit and wait. It's no use working yourself into a frenzy or you won't be fit to see August.'

With great difficulty Jay forced herself to sit still, starting at the slightest sound, and when eventually they heard Jeff she was out of the saloon in a flash. 'What's wrong?' she asked at once. 'Is it serious?'

He smiled and shook his head. 'Not as bad as I expected.'

'Well, come on,' urged Charlie, who had joined them. 'Out with it. What's the matter, and where is he?'

He was aggravatingly slow. 'The old man's wife is

looking after him. He's in their house.'

'Yes, but what's the matter with him?'

'Some local crank of a doctor diagnosed an obscure disease and they were treating him for that, but—well, I'm no medic, but I reckon it's a return of his old complaint.'

Jay shook his arm impatiently. 'What's that? He never told me.'

'I think it's malaria.'

'Will he be all right?' Jay's eyes were wide with fear.

'Of course, and especially now they know what it is and can treat him accordingly.'

'Can't we bring him back here?' said Charlie.

'Oh, please!' Jay added her appeal.

'I think it's best if he stays where he is for a while.'

'But can we see him?' Jay didn't care now what August might think. Her one aim was to be with him, to help him through his illness.

Jeff smiled at her insistence. 'Tomorrow. He's very weak. He needs rest.'

There was one other question that Jay had to put. 'Did—did you tell him I was here?'

Jeff paused significantly then shook his head. 'No. I thought it best not to—in his present state.'

'You mean—you thought he wouldn't want to see me?'

'Not at all, my dear,' laying his arm about her shoulders. 'August is the last person to bear malice. I think he would be more hurt if he knew you were here and didn't go.'

For the rest of the day Jay found it impossible to dismiss the sick man from her mind. The thought of seeing him tomorrow also bothered her. She wanted to, more than anything else, but was afraid of the reception she might get. It was all very well Jeff saying August would want to see her. He did not know all that had gone on between them. Sometimes Jay herself wondered just where things had gone wrong, whether August would have found some other excuse to get rid of her had he not found this most convenient one.

And then it was morning, time for their visit. The village was a mere cluster of white stone houses set in a medly of bright flowers and lush vegetation. Jeff stopped at the last house and Jay felt fear prickle her spine. Was she being wise? Would it be better to stay away? August need never know she had been on the island.

Charlie saw her hesitation and touched Jay's arm, and strengthened by her friend's devotion the girl knew that there was no turning back. She loved this man, and no matter what he said or what he thought her place was by his side. She had more to give than anyone else.

The old man who had first told them about August opened the door. He gave his toothless smile and stood back. Although shabby the house was spotlessly clean. In one corner of the room stood a bed, and it was in this direction that Jay's eyes were drawn.

August was asleep, watched over by the old man's wife. She was small and wizened like her husband, with thick grey hair scraped back into a bun, and she smiled warmly as her visitors approached the bed. 'He sleeps

153

now,' she said haltingly. 'He is much better today. The medicine has done him good. You have not come to take him away?' She looked suddenly apprehensive.

'Not unless you want us to,' assured Jeff. 'I'm sure he shouldn't be moved yet. Please, I would like you to meet my wife, and this is a friend of August's.'

The woman shook their hands warmly. 'You not his wife?' she inquired of Jay, and when she shook her head, 'Not yet, maybe?'

Jay smiled and questioned the woman about his illness.

It appeared that her husband had found him lying on the deck of his boat totally unconscious and running a high temperature. As there were no medical facilities on the island apart from the one man who called himself a doctor their only recourse was to take him back home and get this man to look at him. The fact that he had incorrectly diagnosed August's complaint came as no surprise to Jay as she listened to the woman's tale, and she was thankful that they had arrived at the island when they did, for otherwise August might have died—a thought that brought a shiver to her spine, and automatically she looked at the man who was the centre of her thoughts.

He had woken and appeared to be looking directly at her, yet she was sure he did not see her. His eyes were glazed like a person in a trance. Slowly Jay moved nearer, oblivious now to the other occupants of the room; all her attention focussed on the man lying down. His once tanned face was yellow and drawn; his hair

154

curled damply about his head as though he had recently showered.

Jay felt swift compassion for the man who she had never seen anything else but fit and full of vigour. 'August, can you hear me? It's Jay.'

His eyes flickered slightly then. He licked dry lips and spoke with great difficulty. 'Why are you here?'

'I want to try and help. I thought that——'

He interrupted her, his voice stronger now. 'You should be in England. Why can't you leave me alone?'

Jay's face crumpled. What she had dreaded most was happening.

Charlie stepped forward and tucked her arm through Jay's. 'I brought her, August. It's me who's to blame, if anyone.'

'Maybe so.' He turned his head to the wall, voice muffled by the pillow. 'But I still don't want to see her, ever. Take her away—*now*.'

Jay stared, unable to believe that she had heard correctly, then with a stifled cry ran from the room. Heedless of Jeff calling she raced through the village looking neither right nor left, not stopping until she reached the shelter of the boat.

August hated her!

It was as clear as if he had said the words to her face. What a fool she had been to let Charlie persuade her to join them; even more of an idiot to visit August. Why hadn't she followed her instincts? Instead of which she had suffered the deepest humiliation of all.

Pride forbade Jay to cry, but her eyes ached; her

throat ached—and most of all her heart felt as though it had turned to stone.

Through the port she could see the red sails of *Romany II* neatly furled, the hull and decks had been given a new coat of paint—everything glistened and sparkled. It had that meticulous order about which August was so fastidious.

As if drawn by a magnet Jay climbed off the *Darling* and on to *Romany II*. The hatch opened at her touch and she went down into the familiar saloon. Not a thing was out of place. If August had known he was going to be ill he could not have left it in better shape. Mechanically she lifted the curtain to the forecastle, dropping it immediately when she saw that it had again been converted into a storeroom. It was difficult to believe she had once slept there.

She was still on *Romany II* when Charlie and Jeff returned, but she did not move. She sat quietly in the saloon staring into space and wondering why August hated her so much.

Soon she heard footsteps and then Charlie's head peered through the hatch. 'I guessed I might find you here.' The face disappeared and two trouser-clad legs took its place. Jumping the last few steps, Charlie came and sat beside her friend. 'My poor dear, I am sorry. I can't think what's come over August. It must be his illness.'

Jay shook her head sadly. 'That's how he was once he found out I couldn't crew. We did call a truce, but it never really got off the ground. Let's just say we're incompatible and leave it at that.' It was a hard thing

156

to admit, even to herself, but what other interpretation could she put on his behaviour?

'I don't believe it. Don't forget I know August better than you.'

'Then why don't we get on? Tell me that if you can.'

Charlie spread her hands expressively. 'That's something I don't know, but I intend finding out before we leave this island. Once August's better I shall ask him. He has no right to treat you the way he does.'

'Don't you dare!' Jay looked at her friend in horror. 'This is between August and me. I don't want you interfering, much as I appreciate your concern.' August would never believe Charlie had done it without some encouragement.

'Oh, Jay! Don't you see—in this way we might get to the bottom of the mystery. If he's still got the idea in his mind that he's against all women I'm going to knock it out of him before he goes any further. I'm sure that's what it must be. I can't see any other reason for his attitude. I think he almost let himself fall in love with you and then had some misgivings about the consequences—thus he took the earliest opportunity to pick a quarrel.'

Jay smiled grimly. 'You've got it all tied up. I wish you were right. I'd like it better than anything else in the whole wide world. But he hates me, Charlie, he really does. And I know I'm an ungrateful beast, but I wish you hadn't persuaded me to come back. I wish you'd let me go to England. I might not have been happy, but at least I wouldn't feel so cheap as I do. My pride was still intact.'

'And so it should be now. You're not to take any notice of what August said.'

'As if I can help it,' sniffed Jay. 'I suppose he ran me down still further when I'd gone?'

'No, he didn't. As a matter of fact he said nothing at all, not even to Jeff. He pretended to be asleep and in the end we left.'

'And what do you propose doing now?'

The blonde girl shrugged. 'We can only wait until he's better. We shall visit him, of course.'

While I remain here feeling more and more bitter every day, thought Jay. She was stuck on this island with the knowledge that a further meeting with August was unavoidable. Her cheeks flamed at the idea and she would have given every penny she possessed to find some way out of the situation.

CHAPTER ELEVEN

To fill in the long hours while Charlie and Jeff were visiting August Jay explored the island. She observed with interest the scars in the landscape caused by black lava rock from the lofty volcano; found secluded valleys and rich forests. Everywhere was the scent of flowers, and she discovered that the Romans had called these islands the 'Fortunate Isles' because of their wonderful climate. Had things been different she would have revelled in the exotic splendour of her surroundings. It was so peaceful, so serene, unlike England where even the remote corners were now invaded by holiday-makers.

She had seen no other visitors to this island and the islanders themselves numbered but a few. It was an oasis of calm, but even so did not make up the hurt caused by August's cruel words. And there could be worse to come! Who could tell what would happen at their next meeting? She cringed inwardly at the mere thought.

On the third day of their stay Jeff declared that August was well enough to return to his yacht. Jay paled. The moment she was dreading had arrived. Her love had in no way diminished, every fibre of her being called out for him, but at the same time it made her even more vulnerable and she felt that she could take no more of his insults.

Charlie, observing her friend's sudden change of mood, said, 'Don't worry. He's had time to get used to the idea of you being here—any anger he felt will have evaporated.'

'I doubt it,' returned Jay, and to cover her apprehension, 'I'll go and get his cabin ready.' At least this was a task she would enjoy. A labour of love it could be termed, though she doubted whether August would see it in this light.

She flung open the portholes, polished until everything glistened—not that it really needed this—made up his bed in case he felt tired and on a sudden impulse filled a jug with oleander flowers which grew profusely all over the island. When there was nothing more she could do she decided to go for a walk. The truth was that she wanted to be out of the way when the sea gypsy returned. A foolish notion, she knew, but something drove her on. Far into the island she walked. On her first day she had found a secluded spot and it was to this place she now made her way. It was in the shelter of the hills yet commanded a magnificent view over the azure sea. Golden sunshine, green vegetation and blue waters were her only companions. Even the birds seemed to avoid this spot and she was able to lie back with her eyes closed and let her troubles float away. She could soak up the languid spirit of the island; even pretend that she was one of the islanders herself and that this peaceful existence was hers for all time.

Suddenly through the mists of oblivion she heard her name. Charlie was searching for her. Glancing at her watch, Jay was surprised to find that she had been away for two hours. Sleep had crept up on her unawares and now she stretched her stiff limbs before giving an answering cry.

The other girl came into sight, saying at once, 'What are you doing? I'd begun to think that something was wrong. You're not trying to hide? August was very worried.'

This surprise statement caused Jay to jump to her feet. 'Would you mind repeating that?'

'August was worried,' said Charlie obediently. 'Don't look so amazed. He really was. I told you he'd be different once he'd got used to the idea of you being here.'

'What did he say?' asked Jay next, firmly of the opinion that Charlie had put her own interpretation on August's reaction. He had no doubt inquired as to her whereabouts, but not for personal reasons. It was a natural enough question for anyone to ask.

'He kept asking for you. Said he had something to say.'

Jay nodded grimly. 'I bet he had! And it's not difficult to fathom out what it is.'

'You're away again.' Charlie sounded impatient. 'Only thinking what you want to think. Where's that loving feeling gone?'

Jay shrugged. 'I'm trying to forget it. There seems no point. Oh, come on,' starting down the slope, 'let's get it over.'

'You sound as though you're meeting your doom.'

'I may as well be,' retorted Jay over her shoulder, 'there's no future left.'

Charlie made no attempt to hide her irritability with the other girl and they were still arguing when they reached the boats.

Jeff leaned against the *Darling* puffing contentedly at his pipe. 'August's resting,' he said in response to their questioning looks. 'The walk from the village tired him out.'

'Then I'll not disturb him,' said Jay, her eyes lighting up in relief.

'You won't do that. He's waiting for you. You're to go right down.'

Jay grimaced and with a last despairing glance at Charlie climbed aboard the *Romany II*. At the bottom of the steps she paused. August lay back on his bunk, eyes closed. Jay was aghast at his pallor and fearing he might be asleep prepared to retreat.

'Please sit down. I believe I have to thank you for all this,' indicating the spotless cabin and the flowers on the table. 'Why?'

Jay twisted her fingers awkwardly. 'Because I wanted to.'

'To try and appeal to my better nature? If so I'm——'

'Of course not,' cut in Jay crossly. 'Why do you always think there's a motive behind everything I do?'

'No one does anything for nothing these days.' He sounded bitter and Jay guessed that yet again he compared her with Kate.

'Then you've mixed with the wrong people,' she returned, 'for I've always been taught that there's as much pleasure in giving as receiving, and I never ask for anything in return for what I do.' He really did look tired, she thought, and was sure they shouldn't be arguing. He ought to be asleep, or at least resting quietly. 'I'll go now. I thought you had something to say to me, but I must have been mistaken.'

'I have. Sit down.' and when she had meekly obeyed, 'I would like to apologise for being so rude to you the other day.'

For an instant Jay's heart lifted, before she realised that Charlie must have spoken to him. No doubt she had emphasised Jay's unhappiness and he was now doing this purely to please his blonde friend. 'You don't have to. I quite understand how you felt. I'm sorry you've been ill and I hope you're soon better.' She rose and was halfway up the steps when he called again.

'Jay!'

The girl paused but did not look round.

'I don't like apologies thrown back in my face.'

'In that case you shouldn't say things calculated to hurt,' and she mounted another step.

'*Come back!*'

The words were not to be taken lightly and with some trepidation Jay returned to the middle of the saloon where they glared at each other like animals about to fight. Jay's fingers curled into the palms of her hands and she thrust them into the pockets of her white slacks so that he should not see his high handed manner in any way disturbed her. August himself sat back in his seat, only the beating of a pulse high in his cheek giving away the fact that he was not as relaxed as he seemed.

'Put yourself in my position,' he said. 'What would you think if someone kept appearing on the scene? Would you believe it was coincidental or would you think, like me, that you were being followed—for reasons that were not immediately obvious?'

'I suppose,' said Jay slowly, 'that I'd think like you—but at least I'd give that person a chance to speak up for herself. You always condemn me straight away.'

'I listened to you before, remember? You almost convinced me then, but this time it won't work.'

'But hasn't Charlie explained?'

'Oh, yes, she told me all right. Let's face it, though, if you had an iota of pride you wouldn't have gone with her. It was almost guaranteed that we would meet again.'

'Charlie said not.' Jay's temper was showing signs of getting the better of her. 'Otherwise I wouldn't have come.'

'You expect me to believe that? Really, Jay, you'll have to try much harder.'

'Then you'll have to go on thinking the worst. To think I actually felt sorry for you! I should have hoped you'd die.' With tears blinding her eyes Jay scrambled up the remaining stairs and fled. The fact that he called her back made no difference this time. She had said a hateful thing to him, and it was not as if she meant it. How could she face him after that? She couldn't even face her friends. Back into the island she raced, heed-

164

less of branches clawing at her clothes, intent only on being alone.

She despised herself. August had made an attempt to apologise and she had flung it back at him. Not only that, but she had said an unforgivable thing as well. Who could blame him now for hating her? She deserved all she got.

What had happened to the happy, even-tempered girl she used to be? Did falling in love with the wrong man always result in frayed nerves? It could have been so different had August not taken an instant dislike to her.

When Jay reached her own private place she threw herself down, burying her face in the soft grass and wishing she was a hundred miles away. Had she not been so dependent on Charlie and Jeff she would not have hesitated in leaving the island. Even from Las Palmas she could have flown, but here there was no way of escape. Had she sought the assistance of one of the islanders to row her to Grand Canary she would almost certainly be found out. It was too small a place to do anything in secret. No, she was stuck here and must make the best of it.

After allowing herself time to calm down Jay made her tentative way back to the *Darling*. Jeff was alone. 'Charlie's with August,' he said at once. 'What happened?'

'Do we have to talk about it?' she asked tetchily, 'Let's say August and I will never see eye to eye and leave it at that.'

The big man shrugged. 'If that's the way you feel

I'll say no more. How about something to eat? I'm starving!'

The meal was almost ready when Charlie returned. 'I've asked August to join us,' she said. 'I hope you don't mind.'

Jay's brows rose expressively. 'It's your boat. It's nothing to do with me.'

'Yes, but it's difficult when you're still not friends. But I couldn't leave him to fend for himself. He's still very weak.'

'He told you what happened?'

'Not exactly—he said you accused him of being hard-hearted.'

'Is that all?' and when Charlie nodded Jay felt relief that August had not repeated her odious statement.

Charlie said next, 'You will try and be nice to him? He's feeling rotten.'

'I'll do my best, though if he starts on me I can't guarantee that I'll sit and take it.'

'I don't think he will,' smiled Charlie, 'I've told him a few home truths. Provided you both play your part I can't see there being any more friction. I'll go and fetch him if you're ready. Won't be long.'

Before Jay had time to ask what sort of things she had said to the sea gypsy Charlie had gone. When they returned and took their seats at the table the general conversation took away any feelings of embarrassment that Jay experienced on meeting August again.

The man himself gave no indication that he had been hurt by Jay's hastily spoken words and indeed made every effort to treat her with courtesy. Whatever

Charlie had said had obviously done the trick, thought Jay, though she gained the impression that it was an effort on his part and he would clearly have preferred to leave her out of the conversation.

Nevertheless she too adopted a cordial air and an outsider would never have guessed at the hostility lying beneath their friendliness.

During the days that followed August continued to take his meals with them and Jay felt that gradually he was beginning to relax. They were never alone. Somehow Charlie or Jeff always managed to be present. Whether this was contrived Jay did not know, but she was thankful. Her love for the sea gypsy was, if possible, stronger than ever, but she forced herself not to give away her feelings. For August to know this would be the greatest humiliation of all.

As time passed so too he regained his strength and it was not long before he talked about continuing his voyage. Jeff tried to discourage him, but soon it became all too evident that nothing they could say would alter his decision.

As far as Jay was concerned, one part of her now wanted him to stay, but the strain of keeping up a false relationship was beginning to tell, and she knew it would be a tremendous relief when he had gone.

It was finally arranged that he leave the following Sunday. The next leg of the journey was over two thousand miles to the West Indies, and it was clear that Jeff was uneasy about August attempting this crossing alone. It could take anything from three weeks to two months, and if he should have a relapse——? They all tried not to think about this prospect.

Sunday morning dawned, a bright, clear day when the sun turned the sea into shimmering gold. They were all awake early and through the port Jay watched August making last-minute preparations.

Suddenly she saw Charlie dart across to *Romany II* and begin an earnest conversation with the sea gypsy. From the way they glanced in her direction Jay guessed she was the object of their discussion. Her suspicions were confirmed when Charlie raised a hand and beckoned her across.

'August has a proposition,' said the blonde immediately.

Jay made no attempt to hide her surprise and looked at him wide-eyed.

He appeared to have difficulty in finding the right words and made several false starts before saying, 'As you know, Jeff isn't keen on me travelling alone, even though I've assured him I'm perfectly fit again, so I— er—wondered whether—you'd like to join me?'

This was the last thing Jay had expected. It wasn't possible, not after all that had happened. 'Are you mad?' she asked at last. ''Do you know what you're saying? I'm the girl you threw off your boat because she couldn't crew, remember? I don't know what your idea is, but if you think I'm coming back you're mistaken. We just don't get on together.' It upset her to say these words, but they were true nevertheless and much as Jay would have liked to agree with his suggestion she knew it would never work out.

'Why did you talk me into it?' August said in an

168

aside to Charlie. 'Jay's right, I am mad.'

'So——' it all became clear, 'it was *your* idea.' Jay glared accusingly at the other girl. 'I might have known! Nothing short of a miracle would have caused August to change his mind. I wish you'd consulted me first. It would have saved us both a lot of embarrassment.'

'You're a fool, Jay,' hissed Charlie. 'Why not say yes? It's the perfect solution.'

'To your way of thinking, but not to August's—or mine, for that matter. I'd be no use to him. He'll tell you that himself.'

But Charlie merely smiled. 'You're no greenhorn now. Jeff taught you a lot. I've just been telling August all about it, and he agrees you could be quite an asset.'

'Do you?' Jay looked directly into the dark eyes that gave away none of their owner's feelings.

'In view of the circumstances, I——'

'But you're not keen on the idea?' It was important that she knew the truth. If she thought he *really* wanted her and was not doing it as a favour to Charlie it would make all the difference.

'I wasn't at first——'

'But now?'

He looked at her long and hard before saying, 'I think it might work. Just for this one stretch, of course. After that you'll be free to join up with Charlie and Jeff again.'

Jay did not know what to say. Her heart cried out to accept, but would it be wise? Would she be putting herself in a dangerous position? It was a long journey to undertake with a man who had previously shown strong signs of dislike. There would be no escape if they should disagree. It could prove to be the ultimate end in their relationship. Up till now, Jay was compelled to admit, she had entertained hopes, no matter how slight, of a reconciliation in the not too distant future, but if anything went wrong on this voyage it would be the finish, the complete, irrevocable end. On the other hand there was no reason why things should not run smoothly. She had a certain amount of sailing experience behind her now. They had learned a lot about each other and there had not been a cross word between them for days.

Consequently she made up her mind, though her pulses raced and colour flooded her cheeks when she finally said, 'Okay, I'll come.'

He smiled then, the old familiar smile which reduced Jay to further weakness, and held out his hand. 'Let's shake on it.'

Charlie let out a whoop of joy and raced back to tell her husband.

Left alone, August said, 'I hope you won't regret it. I think perhaps we've both learned a lesson.'

Jay said, 'I would have preferred it to be your own idea. I'm still not convinced that you want me. You've said some pretty nasty things in the past and I don't think I could stand it if you start on me again in mid ocean.'

'Hold on, let's get things straight,' put in August quickly. 'I've not said anything that wasn't justified.

Perhaps I came down on you rather heavily, but you were as much to blame as me.'

If she was not careful Jay could foresee another argument. August was right to a degree, but he seemed to forget the fact that when she strove to justify herself he refused to believe her. Nevertheless she bit back a hasty retort, saying instead, 'Perhaps I was, I'm sorry. The problem now is shall we be able to maintain harmony for the next few weeks?'

'If we both try hard I don't see why not.'

He spoke as though it would be an effort and Jay once again felt that he was doing this more for Charlie's sake than her own. 'If you think the exertion would be too great—I mean, just because Charlie made the suggestion we don't have to go through with it.'

'Meaning you'd like to back out?'

'Meaning nothing of the kind,' she retorted indignantly. 'Why do you always misinterpret everything I say?'

August's eyes twinkled. 'Your hackles are rising, Jay. Sure it's not you who'll find it too difficult?'

About to retaliate, Jay observed his amusement and burst into spontaneous laughter herself. The tension between them was broken and suddenly she felt sure that everything was going to be all right.

An hour later they were ready to sail. They had said goodbye to Charlie and Jeff, promising to meet again in the West Indies. Jay was about to untie the mooring rope when a young boy cycled vigorously towards them waving an envelope.

'For Señor August,' he called.

August thanked the boy and gave him a generous tip, then studied the envelope with interest. Judging by the number of postmarks and addresses it had been following him around for some time. 'There's only one way to find out,' he said, tearing open the flap with his thumb.

The letter was brief and apparently contained bad news, for August's face changed. He looked shocked, thought Jay, watching as he walked to the rail, his companion for the moment forgotten. From the other boat Charlie and Jeff also watched—and wondered.

After a few minute's indecision Jay asked, 'What's wrong? Can I help?'

A long pause before he spoke.

'Kate's dead!'

'Oh, I'm sorry.' Her words were no more than a whisper. Although she had never known August's wife she felt compassion for the man at her side. He was deeply moved by the news.

'A car accident. The funeral was a week ago. I should have been there.' He sounded choked.

'It wasn't your fault the letter didn't arrive in time. In any case, you wouldn't have been well enough.'

'I loved her—once. It was my duty.'

'Please, August.' Jay placed a hand on his arm. 'Please don't blame yourself.'

His lashes were moist when he turned and Jay guessed that although Kate had hurt him he still cared. It was obvious to her that if you loved a person enough to marry them that some shred of feeling would remain, no matter how that person behaved. He would be an extremely hard person to show no emotion at all when he received the news that his ex-wife was dead.

August had proved that he was not as callous as he tried to make out, and this gave Jay renewed hope for the future. At the moment, though, he needed careful treatment. Too much pity could turn him against her as well as not enough.

'What must her family think?' he continued. 'I know I've never kept in touch, but she was my wife once and they did have the decency to let me know.'

Jay had never seen him upset before and it was all she could do to stop herself from gathering him into her arms and murmuring words of comfort. 'Write and explain,' she said. 'I'm sure they'll understand. It's not as if they don't know the sort of life you lead. Come on, let's go below and do it now. I'll take it to the village before we leave.'

As if in a daze August followed her into the cabin. She found pen and paper and while he wrote his difficult letter she went to tell Charlie and her husband what had happened.

Understandably Charlie too was upset. Kate had been her friend as well and it was a shock to hear that she had been involved in a fatal road accident. 'Poor August,' she said. 'I can imagine how he feels. He'll forget all about the way she treated him now and worry himself sick that he wasn't able to attend her funeral.'

'That's why I insisted he write to her parents at once,' said Jay, 'to try and get it out of his system—

173

otherwise he'd worry all the way to Antigua.'

When she returned to *Romany II* August looked more composed and thanked her for being so understanding.

She smiled and picked up the envelope. 'Charlie said she'll see to this. I'll give it to her now and then we can go. You'll feel better doing something.'

He caught her hand as she moved away. 'Jay—I'm glad you're coming. I need you right now.'

CHAPTER TWELVE

AUGUST'S need of her had warmed and strengthened Jay, but ironically she was the one to need him in the beginning. Her old seasickness returned the first night out due to a very squally wind which whipped the waves into a frenzy.

'I really am sorry,' she said as he administered her a tablet that neither of them had thought about earlier. 'I always seem to make a nuisance of myself.'

'It's something you can't help,' he said, surprisingly tolerant on this occasion. 'Try and sleep, you'll feel much better in the morning.'

And she was.

Apart from an occasional bout of nausea she felt almost her usual self and was able to cope with the routine of cooking and cleaning. There was little she could do to help August. The trade winds pushed the vessel along at a good speed and they were both able to relax on the deck and enjoy the thrill of gliding effortless across the waters. August explained to her that many sailors were afraid to attempt this transatlantic crossing. 'It's the great distance that bothers them,' he said, 'Yet with these winds it's more simple than sailing in the tricky English waters.'

'Will it be like this all the way?' not really believing it would.

'Oh, no. We're almost sure to run into a gale, but it can be no worse than any others you've encountered. Jeff told me about your trip from Vigo. You must have been very frightened?'

'I was. I thought we'd never get out of it. But looking back now I'm glad of the experience. I understand a bit more what life at sea is all about.'

August nodded. 'It's not easy, but I for one enjoy it. I think it's the unpredictable that attracts me even more. When I'm in port I feel, what shall I say?— as though there's no challenge; as though life's passing me by. Out here, especially when the weather's bad, it's me against the elements, and so far I've won.'

Even now, just talking about it caused August's face to light up with excitement; his eyes sparkled and he turned to Jay enthusiastically. 'Don't you feel a little bit that way too? Is the sea beginning to get you as it does me?'

Jay gave the question some thought. 'To a lesser degree. I suppose, but I wouldn't like to travel alone, I'd be afraid. When I'm with you it's different. I know I'll be safe.'

August's lips quirked. 'Such faith, you surprise me.'

'I don't doubt your proficiency as a sailor.'

Still more humour. 'It's the other things about me which you suspect?'

'You won't get me going,' said Jay with affected disdain. 'If anyone starts any arguments on this trip it will be you.'

'And as I'm a reformed character we should have quite a peaceful passage.'

It seemed that August was right. For the next few days everything ran smoothly. The weather was in their favour—no cross words passed between them. Indeed, August could hardly have treated Jay with more consideration. There were times when Jay thought that he might be getting fond of her, then there were others when he treated her with indifference, almost as though he was afraid of becoming too friendly. There were other occasions too when she knew he was thinking of Kate for he would lapse into long periods of silence with a frown constantly furrowing his brow. She wished he wouldn't blame himself for not getting that letter in time. After all, Kate had treated him badly; she had turned him against women for ever—as Jay had discovered to her disadvantage. He owed her no loyalty. If he would talk about it he might feel better, but he kept his thoughts bottled up and she felt he would not wish her to intrude.

These periods of silence got longer and longer until some days he hardly spoke at all. Jay began to worry that she herself might have unwittingly done something to upset him, but when she tentatively broached the subject he immediately replied that it was no business of hers. Consequently neither of them spoke very much and the happiness Jay had felt at the onset of the voyage slowly diminished. She resigned herself to playing his game and spent the time writing letters to her parents and logging their journey in a notebook.

After twelve days at sea the fine weather dispersed.

Squalls took the place of sunshine and fair breezes and Jay was now able to help August by reefing in the sails when he instructed or take a turn at the tiller.

One evening when her companion was if possible more morose than ever she decided to tackle him again. 'August,' she said softly, after clearing away their dinner plates and her companion had settled himself with a glass of his favoured Scotch. 'Won't you tell me what's the matter? If it's something I've done I'd rather you say. I know we agreed not to argue, but—well, anything is better than this eternal silence.'

He looked at her with raised brows, then studied the contents of his glass with minute precision. 'I doubt if you'd believe me. In fact, I don't think it would be wise.'

'Who cares about wisdom?' Jay tried hard to control her voice, knowing full well that if she lost her temper at this stage it would get her nowhere. 'I want to know what's wrong—it's as simple as that.'

'And if I refuse to tell you?' He looked at her now, calmly, patiently.

She shrugged and decided that a direct approach was the only way. 'Is it Kate?'

A long pause, then, 'It's you!'

Not surprised, Jay said resignedly. 'I guessed as much. What have I done this time?'

'Nothing.'

This answer *was* unexpected and she looked at him amazed. 'What are you talking about?'

'I'd rather not say.'

'If it concerns me surely I have a right to know?'

178

Jay was perplexed. If she had done nothing to upset him why the peculiar attitude? She was left with no alternative, but to believe that just by being there was sufficient to upset him. 'I think I know,' she said when he did not answer, 'I'm sorry.'

'For what?' It was August's turn to be surprised.

'Intruding on your privacy. I wish Charlie hadn't been so insistent.'

He laughed then. 'Dear Jay! I wish it were so simple.'

This reply put an even more puzzling aspect on the situation. 'Please don't talk in riddles,' she said sharply.

'I apologise. I'm not being fair, but if it will help I'll try to let it bother me any more. I'm very selfish. How about a drink?'

His warm smile caused Jay's heartbeats to quicken painfully and she sat down on the seat opposite before her legs gave way. If only he knew how easily he could make her happy! A smile, a kind word, that was all it needed and the days of torment were erased completely.

She watched as he poured her a dry sherry, saw the concentration on that brown face from which every trace of his recent illness had disappeared, and wished she knew what was on his mind. If only he would give her some indication a clue—no matter how small— so that she knew what caused these moods.

He handed her the full glass but instead of returning to the seat he had vacated he sat down beside her. His thigh brushed hers and Jay's reaction was instantaneous. The touch sent fire coursing through her veins and involuntarily she edged away, missing August's swift frown as she did so.

'To the rest of our voyage.' The voice was non-committal. 'May it continue to be a pleasant one.'

Jay acknowledged his toast with a nod, not trusting herself to speak. This was the closest they had been for the whole journey and it was doing all sorts of peculiar things to her. She marvelled that he had no idea how she felt, for it seemed to her that her feelings must be clear for all to see. Charlie had guessed, and so too had Jeff. It must be the fact that August was so wound up in his own thoughts that he noticed nothing of what was going on around him.

'Penny for them.'

Jay glanced swiftly up. August was regarding her with amusement. 'They're not worth it; they could be of no possible interest to you.'

'Why don't you try me?'

His deep voice teased her and she again felt warm colour flood her cheeks. The power of the man! Why did it have to be like this? If only her feelings did not go so deep.

She shook her head and tried to return his smile, but there was something different about him that made her pulses race, sending electric currents through to her very nerve ends. He was looking as though he had seen her in a new light, as if he had never really studied her before and was surprised by what he saw—pleasantly surprised, for he appeared in a more agreeable mood.

'I have the feeling that you're afraid of me,' he said

gently. 'You need not fear. You're perfectly safe.'

'I'm not afraid.'

'Then why are you trembling?'

'I'm not,' lied Jay bravely. 'There's nothing wrong.'

He leaned closer. 'I don't believe you.'

Jay edged away, but at that moment the boat gave an unsuspected lurch. She fell against August and in so doing spilled the contents of her glass down his shirt.

'Oh, I'm sorry,' she began, when she felt his arms tighten around her. Looking at his face she saw a hungriness; a desire that she had so often wished was there but had been noticeably absent. Even now she thought she must be dreaming, that it was all a figment of her imagination. She had wanted this moment so long that she had interpreted his perfectly natural reaction into her own way of thinking.

When he did not immediately release her she glanced up again. Green eyes met black. Questioning ones met demanding, and then his lips were on hers. It all happened so quickly that Jay had no time to ask herself why.

His kisses were those of a man hungry for love and Jay took what was offered gratefully. She returned kiss for kiss, her fingers mingling in the dark curls and pulling his head closer to hers. When his mouth explored the soft curve of her cheek and the slim column of her throat she made no demur and with closed eyes gave herself up to the ecstasy of the moment.

And then it was over.

Roughly, almost brutally he pushed her away. She

looked at him with startled eyes as he rose and stood with his back to her, one hand to his brow. 'I've done it again,' he said thickly. 'I can't think why. I know it was what you were dreading.'

'But I——' she wanted to assure him, tell him it did not matter.

'No—please. It was despicable of me. I'm going up for some air.' Without looking her way again August strode through the saloon and up the steps.

Jay looked after him for a long time, toying with the idea of following and explaining her own feelings. But, the thought struck her, by so doing she would be putting herself into an even more embarrassing situation. August's kisses had been purely spontaneous, a result of their being thrust together—it was the sort of thing any man would do under the circumstances, and it was a measure of August's decency that he had not allowed it to go any further. It did not mean he loved her, as she would like to think, and therefore it would perhaps be best if she said nothing. Perhaps he would think that her response too had been due to their somewhat unusual situation.

The wind howled and the vessel pitched as the girl rinsed the glasses, but it made no difference to the man above. He remained alone with his thoughts, condemning himself for his impetuous action and no doubt believing that Jay too condemned him.

Suddenly the wind dropped, the sky cleared and all became calm. The setting sun appeared like a big red ball low on the horizon transforming the seascape into an artist's dream. But Jay was unimpressed. Her spirits dropped lower and lower as she realised that this incident would make matters worse. There was little likelihood now that August would maintain their truce.

The taste of his passion had kindled her love and Jay felt very near to tears. His kiss had been everything she expected, lifting her to inconceivable heights, and surely it had not been imagination that August felt this way too? Lust had not been his prime objective, of this she was convinced. He had needed her as she did him.

Eventually she sought the solace of her own quarters, throwing herself down on to the bed. Dear August, she murmured into the pillow, why do I love you so, and why can't you see it? Don't you know you're breaking my heart? The ready tears spilled over and she wept silently. The remainder of the voyage loomed ahead like a nightmare.

Jay did not hear August re-enter the cabin, nor did she know that he was aware of her distress. It was not until a hand touched her shoulder that she sat up with a start.

'August!' Her eyes were wide and luminous, framed by wet, spiky lashes.

'My dear child!' He dropped to one knee beside the bunk and gathered her swiftly into his arms. 'What have I done to you?'

His concern upset her even more and the tears flowed faster. How could he know that his hand which smoothed back her hair was sweet torture? Or the contact between their two bodies set her on fire? She shuddered and lay still, wondering where the end to all this misery lay.

'Please,' he begged, 'please don't cry. I can't bear it. I know I'm to blame, but I didn't mean to hurt you. Dearest Jay, say you forgive me. Let me make it up.'

'August,' he voice muffled against his shoulder, 'it's not what you did—it's——' She stopped. How could she say it was because she loved him? 'It's just that——' Again she paused.

'I scared you? You're afraid it might happen again?' He lifted her chin with one finger and his eyes searched her face. 'Never fear, I won't insult you any more. Here——' he pulled out his handkerchief, 'dry your eyes.'

Jay buried her face in it, glad of the opportunity to hide away from his all too observant gaze. And then she heard words she had never thought to hear; softly, barely discernible, heart-stopping!

'I love you, Jay. I know you'll never think of me in the same way, but I want you to know. I've tried to keep it to myself. God knows I've tried. I've done everything in my power to stop myself falling for you. But you've kept turning up and I can fight it no longer. I'll try not to let it spoil the rest of the voyage, and perhaps, now you know, you won't find it so hard to understand me.'

As he spoke the handkerchief slipped from Jay's fingers. She stared uncomprehendingly, then shook her head. It was all a dream. August wasn't really saying these things. Yet the arm round her was real enough and the eyes that pleaded so eloquently, the face that was ravaged with the pain of love, could be no other than of this world. 'Is—is that why you've been so horrid—because you loved me?'

He nodded miserably. 'I'm a cad, I know, but I can't help it. You're so lovely, so sincere, and I've treated you abominably.'

'Because of Kate?' she whispered hesitantly.

'Yes. I was afraid. Me—the man who travels the world alone, facing unforeseen dangers, often fighting for my life. I was afraid—afraid of a woman—afraid of my own feelings.'

'I do understand, but—but why didn't you tell me?' And save all this heartache, she added silently.

He shook his head. 'I tried to fight it, or more accurately I tried to fight you. If you'd kept away I might have won. Was it really coincidence that made our paths cross on both occasions?'

Jay nodded. 'Though you've never believed me, I'm telling you now that it's true.'

A shadow crossed his face. 'I hoped you'd deny it. A futile wish, I know, but I thought that perhaps you were chasing me, that you might have liked me enough to—to——' He let her go then and turned away. 'Oh, God, I'm stupid! How could any woman want someone like me? What right have I even to ask such a question?'

Suddenly Jay felt like singing. Her face broke into a smile and she swung round on the bed, kneeling behind August and putting her lips close to his ear. 'Go on,' she whispered impishly. 'What was it you wanted to know?' Then she draped her arms over his shoulders and pulled his head back against her breast. Very gently she dropped a kiss on his brow. 'I'm waiting.'

He stopped breathing for an instant, then twisted round to stare at her intently. 'Jay! You don't mean that——'

'I do,' nodding excitedly.

'I can't believe it.'

But when she flung herself into his arms and kisses mingled with tears he was left in no doubt as to her feelings. It was a long time before either of them spoke again and then August said:

'When did you find out? Why didn't you give me some indication?'

Jay pretended shock. 'What, and have you throw it back at me? No, thank you. Your insinuations were bad enough.'

'But don't you see—had I known, none of this need have happened.'

'I'm not so sure. You didn't trust me in those early days. I think you liked me, I think you liked me a lot, but you thought I was another Kate, and had I admitted my love for you it would have made no difference at all. Not until you'd fought and won your own private battle. Do you remember me telling you something like that once?'

'As if I'd forget,' came the laughing reply. 'You were always telling me what was good for me.'

Jay became suddenly serious. 'Except once, when you were ill. I didn't mean what I said then.'

'And I didn't mean it when I told you to leave me

alone. I just didn't like you seeing me like that. I felt humiliated.'

'My darling August, I wanted to nurse you. I wanted to make you better. You hurt me so much when you sent me away—I felt it was the end of the world.'

'We seem to have made a pretty good job of hurting each other,' he said. 'I for one am glad I've come to my senses. What say you?'

Jay rubbed her cheek against his. 'I couldn't have survived another day thinking you hated me. I know I'd have told you in the end how I felt, regardless of the consequences.'

They were silent for a moment, then August said, 'It's a pity.'

'What is?' asked Jay contentedly from her position in the crook of his arm.

'We're in the middle of the ocean. Were we near land we could get married and this trip could be our honeymoon. How does that appeal to you?'

'Very much, but don't captains have the power to carry out a wedding ceremony?'

'I think so, but——'

'Well, you're the captain of this ship, so why——'

'You little witch,' he murmured, 'don't tease me. I might be tempted. You'll have to make do with a wedding in Antigua. We'll fly your parents out—unless you'd rather wait until we get back to England?'

'I couldn't wait that long,' insisted Jay. 'In any case, I'd be frightened. I might lose you—I wouldn't want to do that. You've grown very precious to me.'

'Despite my bad ways?'

'Because of them. I love you, August. I always have and I always will, and I'll do my best to make you happy.'

'And I'll do my share,' he added softly. 'Between us we should have a pretty good marriage.'

Romany II sailed on into the sunset, red sails proud and full, and all was silent in the little cabin below.

Did you miss any of these exciting Harlequin Omnibus 3-in-1 volumes?

Anne Hampson #3
Heaven Is High (#1570)
Gold Is the Sunrise (#1595)
There Came a Tyrant (#1622)

Essie Summers

Essie Summers #6
The House on Gregor's Brae (#1535)
South Island Stowaway (#1564)
A Touch of Magic (#1702)

Margaret Way

Margaret Way #2
Summer Magic (#1571)
Ring of Jade (#1603)
Noonfire (#1687)

Margaret Malcolm

Margaret Malcolm #2
Marriage by Agreement (#1635)
The Faithful Rebel (#1664)
Sunshine on the Mountains (#1699)

Eleanor Farnes

Eleanor Farnes #2
A Castle in Spain (#1584)
The Valley of the Eagles (#1639)
A Serpent in Eden (#1662)

Kay Thorpe

Kay Thorpe
Curtain Call (#1504)
Sawdust Season (#1583)
Olive Island (#1661)

18 magnificent Omnibus volumes to choose from:

Betty Neels #3
Tangled Autumn (#1569)
Wish with the Candles (#1593)
Victory for Victoria (#1625)

Violet Winspear

Violet Winspear #5
Raintree Valley (#1555)
Black Douglas (#1580)
The Pagan Island (#1616)

Anne Hampson

Anne Hampson #4
Isle of the Rainbows (#1646)
The Rebel Bride (#1672)
The Plantation Boss (#1678)

Margery Hilton
The Whispering Grove (#1501)
Dear Conquistador (#1610)
Frail Sanctuary (#1670)

Rachel Lindsay
Love and Lucy Granger (#1614)
Moonlight and Magic (#1648)
A Question of Marriage (#1667)

Jane Arbor

Jane Arbor #2
The Feathered Shaft (#1443)
Wildfire Quest (#1582)
The Flower on the Rock (#1665)

Great value in reading at $2.25 per volume

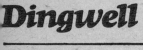

Joyce Dingwell #3
Red Ginger Blossom (#1633)
Wife to Sim (#1657)
The Pool of Pink Lilies (#1688)

Hilary Wilde
The Golden Maze (#1624)
The Fire of Life (#1642)
The Impossible Dream (#1685)

Flora Kidd
If Love Be Love (#1640)
The Cave of the White Rose (#1663)
The Taming of Lisa (#1684)

Lucy Gillen #2
Sweet Kate (#1649)
A Time Remembered (#1669)
Dangerous Stranger (#1683)

Gloria Bevan
Beyond the Ranges (#1459)
Vineyard in a Valley (#1608)
The Frost and the Fire (#1682)

Jane Donnelly
The Mill in the Meadow (#1592)
A Stranger Came (#1660)
The Long Shadow (#1681)

Complete and mail this coupon today!